GAG REFLEX

a livejournal

by Elle Nash

"Elle Nash has always been good at mapping the particulars of unspoken desire."

—Lit Hub

"Relentlessly, whether the scene is a suburban home or an urban sex club, the aura of existential threat is borne."

—Entropy Magazine

"Nash has modeled a portrayal of people operating on the fringes of society."

—Publisher's Weekly

"*Gag Reflex* dragged me back to my worst moments. Nash reflects on the romance of an eating disorder without romanticizing it. *Gag Reflex* is bleak, hardcore and hurts like only a teenage girl can."

**—Tea Hacic, author of *A Cigarette Lit Backwards*
and *Life of the Party***

"Raw and provocative, *Gag Reflex* is less a book than it is a glorious disturbance. It brings me back to the days where I'd scream into a LiveJournal account, only Elle Nash screams beautifully."

—Brian Alan Ellis, author of *Hobbies You Enjoy*

"An itchy, ecstatic recreation of a young woman grasping for meaning and community within a bygone internet, one far more intimate and personal than what exists today. Above all, *Gag Reflex* plumbs the nightmare of possessing a body, being prisoner to a body, the desire to reshape one's body in hope that doing so might also reshape the soul."

—B.R. Yeager, author of *Negative Space*

INDEX.HTML

```
        <TITLE PAGE>
<div class="GAG_REFLEX" index="page"><10>
        <TABLE OF CONTENTS>=id="TOC"</TABLE OF CONTENTS>
              <ENTRIES>
```
```
<div class="FRIENDS_ONLY" index="page"><17>
<div class="SPRING_BREAK_IS_OVER" index="page"><21>
<div class="FUCK_OFF" index="page"><23>
<div class="_" index="page"><25>
<div class="_" index="page"><26>
<div class="CONTRIVANCE" index="page"><28>
<div class="_" index="page"><32>
<div class="UGH" index="page"><35>
<div class="VINDICTIVE" index="page"><36>
<div class="CONFUSED" index="page"><38>
<div class="OH AND" index="page"><40>
<div class="_" index="page"><44>
<div class="_" index="page"><45>
<div class="_" index="page"><47>
<div class="_" index="page"><48>
<div class="_" index="page"><50>
<div class="M." index="page"><51>
<div class="M." index="page"><55>
<div class="SUNY_REJECTED_ME" index="page"><56>
<div class="_" index="page"><57>
<div class="M_AGAIN" index="page"><58>
<div class="LAST_DAY" index="page"><61>
<div class="M" index="page"><65>
<div class="PROM" index="page"><67>
<div class="PLEASE_PULL_THE_TRIGGER_FOR_ME" index="page"><68>
<div class="REGRET" index="page"><70>
<div class="_" index="page"><71>
<div class="ARCHITECTURE" index="page"><72>
<div class="_" index="page"><73>
<div class="_" index="page"><76>
<div class="_" index="page"><79>
<div class="_" index="page"><82>
<div class="THE_STORY_SO_FAR" index="page"><84>
<div class=":(" index="page"><106>
<div class="_" index="page"><107>
<div class="_" index="page"><108>
<div class="_" index="page"><110>
<div class="THUNDER_NIGHT" index="page"><112>
<div class="_" index="page"><113>
<div class="_" index="page"><115>
```

```
<div class="_" index="page"><116>
<div class="_" index="page"><117>
<div class="_" index="page"><118>
<div class="__" index="page"><120>
<div class="_" index="page"><123>
<div class="DON'T_BEAT" index="page"><124>
<div class="_" index="page"><125>
<div class="ADDERALL" index="page"><128>
<div class="WHAT_CAN_BE_SAID_OF_ME" index="page"><129>
<div class="PUBLIC_ENTRY" index="page"><131>
<div class="_" index="page"><134>
<div class="BODY_BELOW_ME_HANG_ON_TIGHT" index="page"><136>
<div class="_" index="page"><137>
<div class="__" index="page"><140>
<div class="__" index="page"><142>
<div class="CIRCUITS_END_WHERE_I_BEGIN" index="page"><144>
<div class="GRAPE_POP" index="page"><146>
<div class="_" index="page"><147>
<div class="_" index="page"><149>
<div class="EACH_YEAR_THE_WEIGHT_CREEPS_UP_..._I_CAN'T_
OUTRUN_THIS" index="page"><150>
<div class="INTRUSIVE" index="page"><151>
<div class="PARADOX_OF_MY_LIFE:_AS_I_SHRINK_I_GET_BIGGER"
index="page"><153>
<div class="_" index="page"><154>
<div class="__" index="page"><158>
<div class="TRIP" index="page"><160>
<div class="BE_THE_MONK" index="page"><164>
<div class="SEPTIC" index="page"><165>
<div class="TANK" index="page"><166>
<div class="WHO_AM_I_?" index="page"><168>
<div class="CONNECTION" index="page"><169>
<div class="_" index="page"><170>
<div class="FUCKK" index="page"><171>
<div class="_" index="page"><172>
<div class="BABY_THIS_IS_WHERE_MY_LIFE_ENDS"
index="page"><173>
<div class="ANIMALS" index="page"><181>
            </ENTRIES>
        <TITLE PAGE>
<div class="ACKNOWLEDGEMENTS" index="page"><185>
        <TITLE PAGE>
<div class="ELLE NASH" index="page"><189>
```

this book is for me,
for my youngerself,
and for my pain

God, in pity, made man beautiful and alluring, after his own image; but my form is a filthy type of yours, more horrid even from the very resemblance. Satan has his companions to admire and encourage him; but I am solitary and abhorred.

Cursed, cursed creator! Why did I live? Why, in that instant, did I not extinguish the spark of existence which you had so wantonly bestowed?

—Mary Wollestonecraft Shelley, *Frankenstein*

GAG REFLEX

XxLUCYS_LIGHT_DREAMxX

[entries | archive | friends | userinfo]

cw/gw in bio

[userinfo | livejournal userinfo]
[archive | journal archive   ]

FRIENDS ONLY

[january 6, 2005 | 06:16 pm]

Quod Me Nutrit Me Destruit

This is a 🔒 'd diary.

[205 comments | post comment]

Comment By: **hungerbound**
2005-03-29 01:46 am (UTC) Select: Edit Delete Screen Freeze Track This

(76.188.116.102)

If you are anorexic, then you do not
need tips on how to not eat.
You do not need to be told how to stop eating.
You do not need to be motivated.

snickers bar
three reeses peanut butter cups
granola bar
cereal bar
milky way bar
five packs of smarties

~~wednesday- fast 6am-6am~~
thursday- 200 cals
friday- fast 6am-6am
saturday- 400 cals
sunday- fast 6am-6am
monday- 600 cals
tuesday- fast 6am-6am
wednesday- 200 cals

XxLUCYS_LIGHT_DREAMxX   [entries | archive | friends | userinfo]

cw/gw in bio

[userinfo | livejournal userinfo]
[archive | journal archive   ]

spring break is over   [march 30, 2005 | 10:05 pm]

today at school, i picked up this ugly pen, and was like, "wow. that's an ugly pen."

"you're an ugly pen," said brian.

"...i'm not really much of a pen," i said.

"well, you're not ugly either, so that insult didn't really work out the way i planned," he said.

"if you say so," i said.

i feel ungrateful for that. but at the same time i don't get it. i'm not fucking not-ugly. sometimes i look in the mirror at my ugly face and pick it apart and it stops making sense. i know what attractive looks like. i am not what attractive looks like.

i know that every once in a while, i'll catch a glimpse of myself in the mirror and it looks okay. it looks normal. average. whatever. but if i look back again, i'm fat. wide. i've got weird eyes that marble out from the sockets and fat cheeks and nasty british teeth that don't come clean no matter how hard i brush them. lips that are drug-house dry. and gross freckles, and bad skin and a big nose, and lifeless, dull hair.

i hate my hair. and that phenomenon where i can take pictures of myself and i can make myself look okay, it's palatable and it's through my eyes. but if someone else takes a picture of me it's disgusting and they say i look fine and all i see are the acne scars on my cheeks and the fat around my eyes. is this how i look through their eyes?

i don't fucking understand it and i feel bad about myself and i'm fat and it's frustrating.

[current music | poison the well - meeting again for the first time]
[8 comments | post comment]

Comment By: **xylitoljen**
2005-03-31 03:36 am (UTC) Select: Edit Delete Screen Freeze Track This
(66.1.243.164)

... *that's not the point, is it? You think people on the outside
give a shit about your sick sense of control? You think they
give a shit about the stereotypes which are obviously based on
some truth? because hey, let's face it, most people don't think
as much as you do and it's a really shallow fucking world. and
for some people, perfection isn't so fleeting.*

*to people on the outside this is something you can get the
fuck over if you really wanted to. if you decided you wanted to
get help.*

but you don't.

*so when do I do what the "GOOD FRIEND" does and let
someone know? so they can force you to get help?*

that's not a threat. it's an honest question.

...

*i'm going to stop here, because i know anything i say will
sound ignorant since i'm not "immersed" in it. deep down, i
want to be the "BAD FRIEND" and tell you it's your body and
your fucked up masochistic little mind. crash and burn, lucy.*

but you know how guilt is such an issue.

...

*Actually, I'm not going to stop. I'M GOING TO KEEP GOING.
Now that we've both established that we don't understand
what the other feels, I'd like to ask an incredibly broad
question!*

What do you want?

XxLUCYS_LIGHT_DREAMxX   [entries | archive | friends | userinfo]

cw/gw in bio

[userinfo | livejournal userinfo]
[archive | journal archive   ]

fuck off   [april 1, 2005 | 11:32 pm]

all i want is to wake up and write poetry in the silence, to
make poetry of my life. instead i slip out of pajamas, pull
the braid out of my hair, listen with urgency as the sounds of
people moving about the house take over.

it's dark and they are terribly alone.'they' quite frankly
contains only two things: my fragile ego and my eating
disorder. there is no other way to speak of this without being
blatant. it is not poetic. as much as i wish it was—desperately
wished somehow that this effort—negative, faithless effort—
tinted the shadows in my skin neon pink and purple, made
me glow. instead, i am quite faithful to the degree these acts
will fix me, fix my mottled, sallow body. bruises on knees.
stomach thick and bloated with dried mango sneakily eaten
in the middle of the night. a violence inside of me which will
never go away. i can never be *that*. that which is ideal. it's
a rejection of it, almost   a statement of what I know i can
never have, what i am not allowed to have. a higher state
of being... beauty, status, well-dressed fashion sense... good
proportions... plastic surgery face.

i will always be striving for an ideal i cannot reach. i will never
escape it, this yearning. i cannot escape society, nor the
expectations of others. i will purge until my insides rot black. it
will always come back. it will always come back.

if reality is objective, i am only what you fucking see

I OBJECT I OBJECT I OBJECT

can't find solace in what is now perceived as lack. i fucking
hate myself. with no remorse. with a violence that shakes. i'm
soft skinned but my bones have hardened. calcium deposited
cartilage, the fat around my heart lithified with the carnage of
constrictors around tiny mice ribs, squeezed till it removes the
soft mealy insides. sucked out by standards i will never reach.
by these industry snakes.

there is nothing but meat inside of me and i can't even honour it; how dare i think i deserve to consume when my flesh isn't even honourable itself; how could one extend honour to the things that nurture if one cannot honour one's own steakish insides.

the cabin has now been depressurized for your comfort. deep sea submarines couldn't save me if they tried.

XxLUCYS_LIGHT_DREAMxX   [entries | archive | friends | userinfo]

cw/gw in bio

[userinfo | livejournal userinfo]
[archive | journal archive   ]

-   [april 2, 2005 | 2:21 am]

*CAN YOU BELIEVE I USED TO BE ELOQUENT LIKE AUTUMN
BREEZE.*

*NOW I AM NOTHING. I AM THE HAGGARD BRANCHES OF
WINTER ASPENS.*

*OH SNOW. OH FROST. PLEASE BLANKET ME SO THAT I MAY
SPARKLE.*

XxLUCYS_LIGHT_DREAMxX   [entries | archive | friends | userinfo]

cw/gw in bio

[userinfo | livejournal userinfo]
[archive | journal archive   ]

-   [april 4, 2005 | 3:45 pm]

today brian told me i had such pretty eyes and
i didnt understand. he told me i had nothing
to be self-conscious about and i didnt understand.
he stared me down. i couldnt look away.
i didnt understand.
he was genuinely nice to me and i didnt understand.
it does not compute.
please do not help.

and i want it all.
so that means i should give it up.

~~sunday- fast 6am-6am~~
~~monday- 200 cals~~
tuesday- fast 6am-6am
wednesday- 400 cals
thursday- fast 6am-6am
friday- 600 cals
saturday- fast 6am-6am
sunday- 200 cals

XxLUCYS_LIGHT_DREAMxX   [entries | archive | friends | userinfo]

cw/gw in bio

[userinfo | livejournal userinfo]
[archive | journal archive   ]

contrivance   [april 4, 2005 | 7:54 pm]

for how long can i push. how much farther. can i test the
limits? the human body is not a smooth running machine
yet i am still robotic. thinking on my feet as fast as i can and
purging out the rest. before my father died he said all my
stress was at the base of my feet. i push it down further into
the dirt and mud, my glazed-over eyes.

i have learned to be as in tune with my body as a guitarist
is with his guitar. when one string is just a little off key i can
feel it. i can tweak it to make the perfect sounds reverberate
through space. i know the difference between one pound less
and one pound more. i know the quickest way to lose bloating
weight and how to clean your insides so well that nothing
comes back up but water.

there are cycles. i want to go on humming. its harder to close
your eyes and ride through the bumps than it is to just accept
that this is what you're doing to yourself. replacing pain with
different pain. duller pain. like balm to burn. i know it is more
than just about weight or feelings. it is how to exist between
living and dying.

when will the human body just break. when can i break. do
i even want to break? there's a point where i get scared. i
mean terrified. i lay in bed, listen to my pulse thread through
my ears, slower than it should be. nails blue. today my hands
tightened up in the shower involuntarily and the world went
dark for a few frames. woke to a bloody nose rinsing down the
drain. the moment when i think i may die, my heart should
be a piston pumping in my ribcage, but it's not. i felt a little
giddy. when the darkness coned in, i thought, *we've arrived*. i
thought, *baby take me away*.

i crawled out of the shower and into my room, more damp
than dry, sweating and clammy on the high pile carpet.
spinning and spinning still. i know i need to consume. but i
cant. and still there are limits as to what the human body can
endure. forty days without food or so it has been said, forty
days between living and dying. when the monk sits on his rock

and closes his eyes. i know this is where i am, too. forty days to heaven.

to the brink of finally conquering the weight.

finally conquering the hunger, the need, the pathetic fucking need when i know goddamn i don't need anything.

nothing can touch me.

that edged lip that sits between living and dying.

on the outside i could probably look attractive.

by attractive i mean thin. and by thin i mean emaciated.

if i even get there.

i am still empty.

is this the feeling i was searching for?

XXkiller_MikeXX (4:43:26 PM): so when are you leaving?

lucifer_dramamine (4:43:29 AM): sometime in june.

XXkiller_MikeXX (4:43:34 PM): when in june?

lucifer_dramamine (4:43:39 AM): i'm not really sure, it depends on if i get accepted at SUNY or not.

XXkiller_MikeXX (1:43:42 PM): ohh. so why are you in such a rush to get out of here?

lucifer_dramamine (4:43:47 PM): idk. this place makes me depressed.

XXkiller_MikeXX (4:44:02 PM): maybe this place makes you depressed bc you never let anyone in it make you happy.

~~wednesday- fast 6am-6am~~
~~thursday- 200 cals~~
~~friday- fast 6am-6am~~
~~saturday- 400 cals~~
~~sunday- fast 6am-6am~~
~~monday- 600 cals~~
~~tuesday- fast 6am-6am~~
wednesday- 200 cals

XxLUCYS_LIGHT_DREAMxX   [entries | archive | friends | userinfo]
                              cw/gw in bio

                    [userinfo | livejournal userinfo]
                    [archive | journal archive   ]

-   [april 5, 2005 | 3:32 pm]

before the cancer, dad said *you don't own the world yet,
because i still do*

small town legends spread their tarantula legs and

web across the country

i will make it to the coastline and drink the atlantic ocean dry

when someday isn't a promise, just a burn fading out

it's hard not to compromise

hungerbound (1:29:53 AM): i can tell you all about the crazy cravings i have
lucifer_dramamine (1:29:57 AM): Tell me.
lucifer_dramamine (1:29:59 AM): We'll share.
XxXDvSxBaBeXxX (1:30:12 AM): yay
lucifer_dramamine (1:30:14 AM): :D
hungerbound (1:30:16 AM): i really like mixing beans and low fat chewy bacon bits and cottage cheese
lucifer_dramamine (1:30:30 AM): I don't like the texture of beans.
hungerbound (1:30:34 AM): i love it
hungerbound (1:30:41 AM): especially with cottage cheese and bacon bits
XxXDvSxBaBeXxX (1:30:41 AM): ohh.
hungerbound (1:30:43 AM): its just right
lucifer_dramamine (1:30:44 AM): I really like mixing cottage cheese with salsa and using that as a dip with tortilla chips.
hungerbound (1:30:46 AM): when they are cold
lucifer_dramamine (1:30:49 AM): mmm.
hungerbound (1:30:55 AM): i also mix up soy sauce and vinegar
XxXDvSxBaBeXxX (1:30:57 AM): i like buttermilk and crackers.
hungerbound (1:30:58 AM): and drink it
hungerbound (1:31:03 AM): mmmm buttermilk is so pungent
lucifer_dramamine (1:31:04 AM): what's buttermilk?
XxXDvSxBaBeXxX (1:31:05 AM): ewww..
XxXDvSxBaBeXxX (1:31:13 AM): um..
XxXDvSxBaBeXxX (1:31:15 AM): well it's milk.
hungerbound (1:31:17 AM): its thick milk
XxXDvSxBaBeXxX (1:31:19 AM): and it's kinda thick
hungerbound (1:31:23 AM): with like... butter chunks in it or something
XxXDvSxBaBeXxX (1:31:27 AM): yea.. it's basically.. old milk.. that's been pasturized(sp)
XxXDvSxBaBeXxX (1:31:29 AM): yea.
hungerbound (1:31:31 AM): it sounds nasty but a tablespoon once in a while is really good

lucifer_dramamine (1:31:32 AM): blaachh. I like skim. Haha. I like when it's like water.

XxXDvSxBaBeXxX (1:31:33 AM): you can get them w/out tho.

hungerbound (1:31:41 AM): it doesn't even taste like milk

XxXDvSxBaBeXxX (1:31:47 AM): i just crunch up or break crackers in a glass.. and pour milk over it and eat it with a spoon.

lucifer_dramamine (1:31:49 AM): I really want a bagel w/ cream cheese.

hungerbound (1:31:59 AM): oh my god i was just thinking of cream cheese

lucifer_dramamine (1:32:01 AM): Oh man!!!

XxLUCYS_LIGHT_DREAMxX   [entries | archive | friends | userinfo]

cw/gw in bio

[userinfo | livejournal userinfo]
[archive | journal archive   ]

ugh   [april 7, 2005 | 10:17 pm]

there are less than 12 weeks or 84 days until graduation.
brian has been passing notes to me in class. the problem
is brian is dating nikita and i don't understand why brian
would keep doing this to me. during third period we have our
computer resource class which really is just a bunch of kids
typing on computers when we already know how to type. brian
likes to sit next to me and whisper in my ear.

lucy it's a bummer you don't want to come over.

lucy i'm slacking on making you feel worthless lately.

lucy you need a good hard reminder of what you mean to me.

lucy i am going to keep you.

then there is mike who is brian's friend. i can't convince myself
mike doesn't know what he is doing, he has to know. during
lunch period, i go to Robertson's class, the newspaper lab,
because it is empty and i can browse myspace or write poetry.
i can Not Eat and no one notices. sometimes i make myself
hot chocolate and have only that for lunch. i don't like to go
to lunch period because i no longer have any friends. they ask
questions about why i choose not to eat or they like to watch
me eat and i do not want to participate anymore. mike must
have followed me to the lab from smoker's corner one day to
find out where i was going. i opened a packet of hot chocolate
and it spilled all over the linoleum floor. when i turned around
to grab the broom from the corner, mike was in the doorway. i
grabbed the broom and the dustpan and got down on the floor
to sweep it up. that's nice, mike said. where a girl belongs. on
her knees.

XxLUCYS_LIGHT_DREAMxX   [entries | archive | friends | userinfo]

cw/gw in bio

[userinfo | livejournal userinfo]
[archive | journal archive   ]

vindictive   [april 8, 2005 | 12:02 am]

part of me wants to fuck mike because there would be a
chance of brian finding out. i know this would hurt him. i
know he wouldn't like it. part of me wants to fuck mike simply
because i know i could if i wanted to, and i just need to be
touched.

today at school we covered how to do our final portfolios
in class. graduation is coming up in less than four weeks.
during lunch i went back to newspaper lab, hoping mike
might follow me there again. he did not. i signed on AIM
hoping hungerbound was on, but she wasn't. and Jenny and
I are fighting right now and she won't talk to me. i think she
reported me to the counselor. the other day i passed through
the hallway and Mrs. Hanover stopped me and she put a hand
on my shoulder. she squeezed it, my shoulder, in her hand.
she said, are you alright? you're looking thin lately.

i just laughed at her. i haven't lost any weight in weeks. i
know someone must have tipped her off.

[2 comments | post comment]

wednesday- fast 6am-6am
thursday- 400 cals
friday- fast 6am-6am
saturday- 900 cals
sunday- 400 cals
monday- 600 cals
tuesday- fast 6am-6am
wednesday- 200 cals

XxLUCYS_LIGHT_DREAMxX   [entries | archive | friends | userinfo]

cw/gw in bio

[userinfo | livejournal userinfo]
[archive | journal archive   ]

confused   [april 8, 2005 | 11:23 pm]

after school i drove to work, and there was a wooden block
in the road. i thought i could drive over it so it would pass
under my car. instead it hit my front left tire which popped. i
left my car at a taco joint and walked the rest of the way to
work. brian texted how was i, and i told him what happened.
at 8:45, he showed up at radioshack to take me home. jenny
let him stay in the store even after closing. he ran his hands
through his dark hair. the bottom of my feet and tips of my
fingers tingled with numbness or excitement. sometimes,
when you go long enough without eating, the body starts to
shut off your extremities. the tip of your nose gets cold.

brian took me in his saturn to drop me at my car. he even got
out and helped me put on the spare tire. the spare was flat.
we realized the back left tire was flat, also.

i told him not to help me but he did anyway. i kept asking him
why. why do you want to help me. i can just call my mother
and she'll come get me. when brian was jacking the car up,
he kept scraping his knuckles against the ground. it was cold
outside, and the tip of my nose was going numb, one of my
legs, too. i panicked a little. i thought, there isn't enough meat
on my body. i kept thinking of what brian's chest must have
felt like beneath his parka, emitting all that heat. i'm so sorry,
brian, i said. you know you don't have to do this for me. he
told me to shut up. little clouds of air puffed from his mouth.
you didn't ask for help, he said, i offered. so take it.

brian drove me home. at the end of the driveway there was a
pause and i knew he was waiting for something. if nikita found
out she might fight me, i thought. she was bigger than me,
taller. she was more voluptuous. when brian leaned forward,
i imagined her fist hitting my dogtooth, both my tooth and
her fist drawing blood. i pulled back. i wanted him to kiss me,
to ignore my body language and just go for it, but instead he
said goodnight and sorry we couldn't fix the tire. i got out and
went straight to my room.

later, beth from work called and said her boyfriend, steve, was on his way to pick me up to pump air in the tires so i could at least drive my car home. the back tire is fucked. air kept leaking out really fast. my car is still at the taco joint.

people care about me. i don't understand it.

i am going to call the tow truck company tomorrow morning and then get my tires sorted out. this means no therapy appointment tomorrow. wednesday instead.

i was upset and ate my way into oblivion, and took laxatives. i suck. whatever.

i am glad i do not work until saturday. i hate life and i hate work and i hate me at the moment. i can sort of crawl into my mind for a couple days without worrying.

i did not step on a scale today, though. first time in months.

XxLUCYS_LIGHT_DREAMxX   [entries | archive | friends | userinfo]

cw/gw in bio

[userinfo | livejournal userinfo]
[archive | journal archive   ]

oh and   [april 8, 2005 | 11:54 pm]

the other day brian said, "i wish my girlfriend was as smart as you, lucy."

i came home and listened to Otep's 'Blood Pigs' on repeat for two hours, processing. the way her anger sounds outside of language, every time i listen i memorize a new line. wish i could turn my pain over the way she does, tumble it until it was something pristine and presentable. a poem, a sentence, a paragraph doesn't hit the way her throttle hits me. would it ever? how could i compact my pain into something so tender and beautiful it doesn't even need words to be expressed?

what i want to hear from brian: "you can trust me and feel safe with me."

he doesn't feel safe. no one does.

it's fruitless for him to say things like that. he could leave his girlfriend. he tells me he wishes he could make her grow up, but all they do is feed off each other's negative energy.

[current music | what comes around - ill niño]
[16 comments | post comment]

wednesday- fast 6am-6am
thursday- 400 cals
friday- fast 6am-6am
saturday- 900 cals fast 6am-6am :)
sunday- 400 cals
monday- 600 cals
tuesday- fast 6am-6am
wednesday- 200 cals

hungerbound (1:32:05 AM): i like REALLY garlicy cream cheese
lucifer_dramamine (1:32:05 AM): You know what's soo good??!
hungerbound (1:32:13 AM): no bagel ... i just want it so strong i kill people with my breath
XxXDvSxBaBeXxX (1:32:17 AM): ... i love cream cheese. -_-
lucifer_dramamine (1:32:53 AM): When I binge.. I'll take a tortilla, spread some cream cheese on it, all thick.. and then put bacon slices in it. And wrap it up and microwave it for like 30 seconds. Oh god.
hungerbound (1:33:00 AM): oh mmmmmm
XxXDvSxBaBeXxX (1:33:03 AM): oO that sounds yummy.
hungerbound (1:33:04 AM): bacon and cream cheese
lucifer_dramamine (1:33:07 AM): Yeah.
hungerbound (1:33:19 AM): dude. if i want something fatty
XxXDvSxBaBeXxX (1:33:20 AM): i like cheez itz with italian dressing poured on top. i eat it teh same way i do buttermilk and crackers.
lucifer_dramamine (1:33:29 AM): Holllyyy shit. Lol. It's soo good. I haven't had it in like 6 months.
hungerbound (1:33:29 AM): YEAH
hungerbound (1:33:33 AM): italian and
hungerbound (1:33:37 AM): cottage cheese
hungerbound (1:33:38 AM): and bacon
lucifer_dramamine (1:33:41 AM): Mmmm.. cheez its.
lucifer_dramamine (1:33:45 AM): I've never liked dressings for some reason
XxXDvSxBaBeXxX (1:33:51 AM): my mom has a habit of eating weird stuff.. so i got that from her.
hungerbound (1:33:52 AM): or... italian dressing... and mushed up potato ... and sour cream and bacon
hungerbound (1:34:00 AM): i eat such bland food
XxXDvSxBaBeXxX (1:34:04 AM): she adds the strangest things together. i'd swear she was pregnant if she hadn't had her tubes tied.
hungerbound (1:34:05 AM): but i fantasize about crazy shit
lucifer_dramamine (1:34:12 AM): You know what's really good, too?
lucifer_dramamine (1:34:15 AM): My dad eats this.

hungerbound (1:34:25 AM): dude, you guys, this is the best convo ever
XxXDvSxBaBeXxX (1:34:29 AM): lol
lucifer_dramamine (1:34:35 AM): Take like a hot dog bun, and put mayo on one side, and peanut butter on the other. and then a hot dog. OMG ITS SO GOOD.
hungerbound (1:34:39 AM): ...
lucifer_dramamine (1:34:39 AM): You know, it really is.
hungerbound (1:34:43 AM): that is NASTY
lucifer_dramamine (1:34:46 AM): LOL
XxXDvSxBaBeXxX (1:34:47 AM): eww. lol
hungerbound (1:34:52 AM): although
lucifer_dramamine (1:34:54 AM): It's really not. You have to try it before you judge it.

XxLUCYS_LIGHT_DREAMxX   [entries | archive | friends | userinfo]

cw/gw in bio

[userinfo | livejournal userinfo]
[archive | journal archive   ]

\-   [april 11, 2005 | 6:33 am]

some people want to feel free now.

i want to feel free in the future.

XxLUCYS_LIGHT_DREAMxX   [entries | archive | friends | userinfo]

cw/qw in bio

[userinfo | livejournal userinfo]
[archive | journal archive   ]

-   [april 12, 2005 | 3:36 pm]

god what am i doing

like i dont even want to go to therapy anymore because i know
shes going to make me face who i am

just some dumbfuckign crybaby that cant handle anything
because i cant face myself so im just going to run away

because thats what i do with everything

and i do this all to myself and i want to stop it and i know i can
but i fucking wont

and its like i dont even have a real problem because even my
therapist said that i have so much success in my life and there
is no proof of this self destructive nature i speak of

she said *i want you to prove to me that you are this self
destructive person*

i dont want to do this anymore

[8 comments | post comment]

wednesday- fast 6am-6am
thursday- 400 cals
friday- fast 6am-6am
saturday- fast 6am-6am :)
sunday- 1300 cals
monday- 980 cals
tuesday- 800 :(
wednesday- 200 cals

XxLUCYS_LIGHT_DREAMxX   [entries | archive | friends | userinfo]

cw/gw in bio

[userinfo | livejournal userinfo]
[archive | journal archive   ]

-   [april 12, 2005 | 6:45 pm]

this week has been shit and i've been eating at least 1000 calories a day. fuck. i know i will not drop any weight by prom unless i start fasting hardcore.

i wrote this thing in my other public livejournal and jenny saw it and got angry. she doesn't understand. people get frustrated when they can't comprehend.

things are tense/awkward now in newspaper class. i wonder if anyone else knows. jenny would talk, i think.

during layout night, they said some hurtful things. but not directed at me. i know pro-anorexia is fucking dumb. i am not particularly pro-anorexic. i am just pro-not-ignorant. i don't know. or care anymore. they are going to order pizza tonight in layout. i need to find out how many calories are in pizza. shit. i can't not eat because Robertson might think something. only white rice from friday night layout? no food tonight? he was surprised i was just getting rice. i guess i'm "not eating" until tonight then. i feel so bloated and full. i want to try and find some phentermine to buy. or jenny has adderall but she might not sell to me now.

XxLUCYS_LIGHT_DREAMxX   [entries | archive | friends | userinfo]

cw/gw in bio

[userinfo | livejournal userinfo]
[archive | journal archive   ]

-   [april 13, 2005 | 5:45 am]

nothing to die for here, just here to die

hungerbound (1:34:57 AM): my friend takes the movie hot dogs
XxXDvSxBaBeXxX (1:34:58 AM): i like banana and peanutbutter sandwhiches.
XxXDvSxBaBeXxX (1:34:59 AM): whoa..t ypos
lucifer_dramamine (1:35:08 AM): mmm. with honey and marshmallow spread.
hungerbound (1:35:11 AM): and then fills up the container with the popcorn butter
XxXDvSxBaBeXxX (1:35:14 AM): or banana and mayonaise.. but haven't had it in yaers.
hungerbound (1:35:19 AM): EWW.
hungerbound (1:35:28 AM): mayo is the nastiest thing ever. i can't touch it unless its with tuna
lucifer_dramamine (1:35:30 AM): I haven't tried that.
XxXDvSxBaBeXxX (1:35:35 AM): oO
lucifer_dramamine (1:35:37 AM): Lol!! I like mayo, I get it from my mom.
XxXDvSxBaBeXxX (1:35:46 AM): ya.. that's about the only thing i'll eat it with.. aside from scrambled egg sandwhiches.
hungerbound (1:35:51 AM): yick
XxXDvSxBaBeXxX (1:36:09 AM): i've taken mayo out of any sandwhich i eat. it's just... -gag-.
hungerbound (1:36:09 AM): i love egg beaters with bell pepper though
hungerbound (1:36:09 AM): oh my gosh its SO mmm
lucifer_dramamine (1:36:11 AM): Mmm. a bacon egg and cheese sandwich slathered with mayo.
hungerbound (1:36:16 AM): D:
XxXDvSxBaBeXxX (1:36:18 AM): -gag-
lucifer_dramamine (1:36:19 AM): eggbeaters is so excellent.
hungerbound (1:36:20 AM): DUDE UR SO NOT ANA
lucifer_dramamine (1:36:24 AM): LOLZ.
XxXDvSxBaBeXxX (1:36:24 AM): i like drinking pickle juice.
XxXDvSxBaBeXxX (1:36:27 AM): i wish they sold it in stores.
hungerbound (1:36:28 AM): me too!

XxLUCYS_LIGHT_DREAMxX   [entries | archive | friends | userinfo]

cw/gw in bio

[userinfo | livejournal userinfo]
[archive | journal archive   ]

-   [april 19, 2005 | 2:46 pm]

screaming evanescence at the top of my lungs, after school
before anyone is home, gives me a raging hard on.

[0 comments | post comment]

XxLUCYS_LIGHT_DREAMxX　　　　　　　　　[entries | archive | friends | userinfo]

cw/gw in bio

[userinfo | livejournal userinfo]
[archive | journal archive　　]

M.　　　　　　　　　　　　　　　　　　[april 20, 2005 | 7:33 pm]

i'm in love with someone who isn't brian and it hurts so much.

its been a long long time.

~~thursday- fast 6am-6am~~
friday- 800 cals
saturday- 700 cals
sunday- 600 cals
monday- 400 cals
tuesday- 600 cals
wednesday- 800 cals
thursday- 700 cals

x2djunglist (8:44:18 PM): i heard you gonna screw some guy next weekend

lucifer_dramamine (8:44:41 PM): yeah, if i can get over there

x2djunglist (8:45:10 PM): have fun i guess *laughs at you*

lucifer_dramamine (8:45:29 PM): o.O? ok? why laugh at me?

x2djunglist (8:45:59 PM): cuz. i find things like that funny. have fun *holds in laugh*

lucifer_dramamine (8:46:51 PM): yr an asshole, you know that?

x2djunglist (8:47:39 PM): why am i an asshole

lucifer_dramamine (8:48:00 PM) bc you lied to me about loving me and lots of other things.

lucifer_dramamine (8:48:03 PM): i could go on, trust me.

x2djunglist (8:48:18 PM): riiiiight

lucifer_dramamine (8:48:38 PM): yeah i know i'm right

x2djunglist (8:49:03 PM): well i didn't lie. i thought i did. but i didn't. sooo yeah

lucifer_dramamine (8:49:38 PM): i noticed how you were so "in love with me" when you wanted to get me in bed, but then all of a sudden you werrent

x2djunglist (8:50:04 PM): no. i loved you

x2djunglist (8:50:06 PM): dont talk about that my parents are around

lucifer_dramamine (8:50:24 PM): you said real love never dies....

x2djunglist (8:50:59 PM) then i never had real love. i THOUGHT i loved you

lucifer_dramamine (8:51:14 PM) you don't even know what love is

x2djunglist (8:51:14 PM) yeah i do. whats yur problem

lucifer_dramamine (8:52:05 PM): YOU being an ASS

x2djunglist (8:52:15 PM): ohhhh that really sucks

x2djunglist (8:52:33 PM): for you

x2djunglist (8:52:56 PM): your always complaining about me

lucifer_dramamine (8:53:56 PM): yeah cuz i don't like you

x2djunglist (8:55:37 PM): god your dumb.

x2djunglist (8:55:54 PM): your the dumbest person i've ever met

x2djunglist (8:56:16 PM): i laugh at you
x2djunglist (8:57:08 PM): you have halatosis
lucifer_dramamine (8:57:30 PM): that's what toothbrushes are for. you should really learn to use one.
x2djunglist (8:58:14 PM): wow
x2djunglist (8:58:18 PM): hey i do
x2djunglist (8:58:21 PM): my teeth were rotted by my braces so that doesn't hurt my feelings
x2djunglist (9:01:29 PM): tramp
lucifer_dramamine (9:01:39 PM): can't think of anything else, huh?
x2djunglist (9:02:02 PM): no, i'm not gonna waste my time on a maggot like you
lucifer_dramamine (9:02:16 PM): then why are you wasting yr time calling me names?
x2djunglist (9:02:41 PM): tramp and maggot wooooo 2 names
lucifer_dramaine (9:02:58 PM): does that make you feel like a big boy?

XxLUCYS_LIGHT_DREAMxX   [entries | archive | friends | userinfo]

cw/gw in bio

[userinfo | livejournal userinfo]
[archive | journal archive   ]

M.   [april 21, 2005 | 12:33 am]

forever is not real. there is no hope for that.

XxLUCYS_LIGHT_DREAMxX   [entries | archive | friends | userinfo]

cw/gw in bio

[userinfo | livejournal userinfo]
[archive | journal archive   ]

SUNY rejected me   [april 22, 2005 | 8:13 pm]

I AM STILL HERE AND UPSET THEREFORE I CANNOT STOP
TYPING IN CAPS LOCK. FUCK.

EVERY TIME I REACH OUT TO GRAB REALITY IT SWINGS
AWAY ON ITS PENDULUM, LAUGHING.

I FLOAT ON A SWINGING ROPE IN OUTER SPACE AND TIME.
WHERE IS MY REALITY.

I KEEP HAVING INSANE UPS AND DOWNS. NIGHTS SPENT
DRINKING COFFEE FOR HOURS TILL THE SUN RISES AND
STILL LIVING. DAYS SPENT CRASHING MY FISTS INTO
MIRRORS AND SQUEEZING THE EXCESS OF MY BODY TILL I
BRUISE ACCORDINGLY WITH MY WHITE FINGERTIPS.

OVER-ANALYSIS IS KILLING MY BRAIN. I WANT TO LEAVE
THIS EARTH, MY SPACE SHIP HURTLING THROUGH STICKY
RED VEINS UNTIL WARM PUNGENT REGRESS.

[4 comments | post comment]

XxLUCYS_LIGHT_DREAMxX   [entries | archive | friends | userinfo]

cw/gw in bio

[userinfo | livejournal userinfo]
[archive | journal archive   ]

-   [april 26, 2005 | 11:42 pm]

i'm sorry i'm sorry this will be my
first night sober since
last tuesday today i
purged dinner but i'm not
going to let it set me back

<flab.jpg>

i wanna lose just like five pounds

XxLUCYS_LIGHT_DREAMxX   [entries | archive | friends | userinfo]

cw/gw in bio

[userinfo | livejournal userinfo]
[archive | journal archive   ]

M again.   [april 27, 2005 | 12:33 am]

i guess i should explain.

skipped school the last couple days, hanging out with mike.
yes, that mike.

it's hard to describe my wanting... at night when i'm not with
him i'm thinking of what it feels like to run my fingers through
his hair, or what his face looks like squinted together with him
inside me. mike has his own apartment; he turned 18 in first
semester and moved out immediately. mike invites me over
to drink beer and watch south park. the first day i went over,
there were other boys there, but they weren't boys that went
to our school. i didn't know them at all. i sat on the couch
quietly texting Jenny the whole time, waiting for the boys to
leave. when it got late enough, after three beers, mike got
up and went into his bedroom wordlessly. i froze, and waited
a moment to see if he would come back, to come get me. i
wasn't sure what he was doing, or what he wanted. the entire
time south park played he hadn't said a word to me. i kept
thinking about brian's whispers.

lucy it's a bummer you don't want to come over.

lucy i'm slacking on making you feel worthless lately.

lucy you need a good hard reminder of what you mean to me.

lucy i am going to keep you.

i got up and left, rejected and confused. walked home through
the apartment complex, into a subdivision, over a small
concrete bridge and into my subdivision. even though it was
dark and i was alone there were street lamps and i wasn't
afraid. i peeled open the door to my house slowly, crept
into the kitchen and turned my shirt into a basket. i stuffed
everything i could find in there, went upstairs to my computer,
logged onto AIM, and talked with hungerbound for a while.

he is so fucking hot. fuck.

i ate one hostess cake. i drank a liter of milk. i cried. i threw it
up. hungerbound talked me down. i took photos of myself in
the bathroom, sucking in my stomach like a wanarexic loser.
i pinched myself, i burned my arm with a lighter. the scab is
yellow now, i think it's infected. i haven't lost any weight in
weeks.

the second day i went over, mike and his boys were there
again. i held my stomach in my hands, bloated from the beer.
this time when he went into his bedroom, after everyone left,
i got up and followed. mike was laying in bed already, the
room darkened by a blanket pinned over the window. i got
in his bed, him beneath the blankets and me above. i was
still clothed, my sneakers pulled against the comforter. it was
quiet, but you could hear the sounds of construction crews
outside. mike didn't move at all. i put my hand around his
waist, kissed the back of his neck.

mike whispered, "what about brian?"

i asked, "what *about* brian?"

i waited for an answer. instead of silence, mike was out,
snoring. i got up and went home.

lucifer_dramamine (10:23:15 PM): OMG. I hung out at his house yesterday. But I didn't know to like... make any moves LOL

lucifer_dramamine (10:23:15 PM): I don't know how to tell him he's hot without being like... you're hot.

hungerbound (10:23:31 PM): don't tell him he's hot— don't

hungerbound (10:23:35 PM): it'll inflate his head

hungerbound (10:23:47 PM): trust me boys are cocky esp since he was pretty darn cocky at the beginning of the semester

hungerbound (10:23:42 PM): just be like I like you and I think you're really attractive

lucifer_dramamine (10:24:32 PM): but what if the feeling isn't mutual

lucifer_dramamine (10:24:42 PM): I totally can't tell

lucifer_dramamine (10:24:47 PM): he's so fucking smart ah!

lucifer_dramamine (10:25:01 PM): I don't want him to think it's petty

hungerbound (10:27:26 PM): o ish

hungerbound (10:27:29 PM): he likes you he does!

hungerbound (10:27:33 PM): you said he was looking at you continuously

hungerbound (10:27:38 PM): you hung out w him?

hungerbound (10:27:41 PM): he's totally into you. you're SMART

Last day   [april 27, 2005 | 1:16 am]

i couldn't tell if mike was fucking with me or not. every morning last week he texted me: *Skip?*

the weekend came and went. brian messaged me on AIM a few times but mostly was with nikita. i wrote poems. i tried to think about something my therapist said, about considering why i choose to go after the men i go after: emotionally unavailable. have girlfriends. whatever.

i'm on medication now. i also started taking diet pills with hoodia, so i hope they work. for some reason, i feel like binge eating so bad, i feel like cutting, too. it feels so pre-teen to cut, but i get these intrusive thoughts, that i should just do it, just slice right down my leg with a piece of glass. it would feel so good to look at the meat inside me. all that pink and white striation, like a layer cake. i have eaten one cookie and half a donut. i feel so alien in this house. I sometimes wish eating disorders were easier to understand from the outside. how do you explain to someone you can't eat a piece of fruit or cracker for fear of gaining weight? how do you explain to someone that one of your ultimate desires is to look like a fucking skeleton?

last night dragged on. i don't know how i'll make it through tomorrow. mike wants me to come over today because his new girlfriend is out of town, but if i go, it means i might not see anyone again until graduation, if that. my mother has been unbearable all week, and i hate being here (earth) with her alone without dad to run interference. she interrupts me when i speak my mind about anything so i stay quiet. she makes me out to be this ungrateful little child in front of everyone. she came to speak to my teachers yesterday for some open house, making snide remarks the whole time. "she doesn't act that way at home, let me tell you." i cannot stand it. i do not want mr. robertson to think i am immature and ungrateful. i feel like i might as well not go to class. everyone would be happier. i am not supposed to vomit on purpose while i'm on this medication but i should do it anyway. have a seizure. hope it all ends.

my ultimate goal weight was XX for a while but that number feels too large now, and i'm cutting it down to XX. cutting, cutting. it feels right, i sort of can't wait for the summer because i am starting a detox diet coupled with a juice fast. i think i am about XXX right now. i can get away with eating one meal today and a piece of fruit and one meal tomorrow. graduation will be whatever. my mom will take me out to eat with her friends to celebrate and after i'll get back to it. i miss when i could restrict for days, weeks on end. i don't know what happened to my control. i need to make small goals again. i would like to be XXX by the 30th. i don't want to start my fast off at a high weight because anything i lose won't get me below XXX.

lucifer_dramamine (03:33:15 AM): okay hit me
hungerbound (03:33:31 AM): ok ready
lucifer_dramamine (03:34:04 AM): yes
hungerbound (03:34:15 AM): taste is a temporary desire.
When you satisfy it, it only grows. Thin is a constant desire.
When you satisfy it, it only shrinks
hungerbound (03:34:18 AM): thin is a skill
hungerbound (03:34:25 AM): an imperfect body reflects an
imperfect person
lucifer_dramamine (03:35:57 AM): fuck
hungerbound (03:37:26 AM): pain is only as real as you
allow it to be
hungerbound (03:37:32 AM): calories can't make you happy
hungerbound (03:37:38 AM): if you want food, look in the
mirror at your thighs (ok but yr thighs are perfect uwu)
hungerbound (03:37:42 AM): hearts live by being wounded
hungerbound (03:37:49 AM): there can be no reality to the
things you want unless you have structure in your mind first.
The word is control. If you can dream it, you can do it.

~~friday- 800 cals~~
~~saturday- 500 cals~~
~~sunday- 300 cals~~
~~monday- 200 cals~~
~~tuesday- 600 cals~~
~~wednesday- 600 cals~~
~~thursday- 100 cals :)~~
friday - 200 cals

cw/gw in bio

[userinfo | livejournal userinfo]
[archive | journal archive   ]

M   [april 28, 2005 | 10:11 pm]

in the morning i stopped at smoker's corner to see everybody,
jenny was there, too. when first bell rang i walked up the
street, hoping the school cameras wouldn't catch me leaving,
and headed toward's mike's apartment, fantasizing about
what was going to happen. i put The Nameless by Slipknot on
repeat the whole thirty minute walk, so desperate for intimacy
that i imagined M making me cry. in my fantasy, i wanted him
to tease me to frustration, making me feel good and then
taking it away. over and over again. i wanted to want him
so badly i would burst into tears. then i imagined his body
hovering over mine, asking if i was okay. the softness in his
eyes, that's what i wanted. something brutal making space for
me. i saw myself nodding yes.

as i walked a thunderclap heightened my anxiety, took me
out of the fantasy. i found myself too needy, wanting him
near me. when it got to the chorus for the tenth time i turned
around and walked towards home for a minute, too scared to
admit what i wanted. i didn't want to face it. but i didn't want
to go home, either. i changed my mind again. i made it to his
apartment. his room smelled like weed. he took off his clothes
and looked dull and brutish in the low light. built but doughy.
like he was working his way toward it. strong, thick arms like
fat, truck-length forest snakes. a divot that ran through the
center of his forehead—that main vein pulsing—furrowed all
the time. closer to animal than man.

i felt hit by the risk of this venture. what if the sex was bad?

he put his hand on my chin and squeezed and i felt nothing,
like when i purge. completely lost, brainless, the way a log or
a chair might feel. i want that feeling all the time.

i went down on him for what seemed like an hour. my gag
reflex dead. he pushed past the glottal stop and made
incredulous noises. "for such a young girl you suck dick so
good."

i stifled a laugh while he was in my throat, because i imagined him fucking older women when he said that, like cougars, soccer moms, then i saw mike for who he was—just this boy. this boy who wanted to play at adult. who wanted mommy to take care because he'd never had it. mommy-starved. i understood. i am mommy-starved, too. my mood dropped because i saw myself on the flip side of it. i was looking for a place to feel safe. when my brain is emptied of thoughts, then i feel safe.

i kept going. spit thick and bubbling at the side of my lips. then he came, and i swallowed (between 5 and 25 calories per teaspoon, zinc, fructose, protein, vitamin b12).

after that, i felt cleansed.

will straight men ever know the true zen of giving a blow job?

XxLUCYS_LIGHT_DREAMxX   [entries | archive | friends | userinfo]

cw/gw in bio

[userinfo | livejournal userinfo]
[archive | journal archive   ]

prom   [april 29, 2005 | 3:54 pm]

today was the cinco de mayo assembly at school. i had no friends to sit with. lol. still trying to liquid restrict. liquid restriction if anything lets me eat less. keeps me from eating so much.

prom is may 8 or 7. i can lose some weight by then. i know i can if i keep this up.

i want mike to ask me.

i just want to be in love and have it be okay. i want to run away. i'm afraid to love but i want connection. i also am sick of my wormbaby needs.

at the moment, i am mentally sicker than i've ever been. i feel disgusting. giving in to the weakness of the flesh.

destroy the body to lose the mind.

maybe i should just recover. i'd deserve that torture. that would be the true masochism. weight gain, ripping away all my lovely coping mechanisms. wouldn't that be a treat.

[current music | brand new love - deadsy]
[8 comments | post comment]

cw/gw in bio

[userinfo | livejournal userinfo]
[archive | journal archive   ]

please pull the trigger for me   [may 5, 2005 | 1:16 am]

I HAVE THE HEALTHY BODY. or so it would seem. my hair is
now shit, my bowels fucking hate me and my digestive system
is disagreeable. I FEEL LIKE I HAVE BEEN EATING HEALTHILY
OR WHATEVER FOR SO LONG and in reality it has only been
since like, the beginning of MAY.

but i do this a lot. these dumbass periods of self-recovery.
i'm too chicken-shit to stay sick but at the same time i'm too
chicken-shit to stay healthy as well.

i stepped on the scale and saw an ungodly number. i will not
repeat it.

once you've gotten under XXX pounds, anything above that is
too excess. it's funny because my first ever long term goal of
XX (which was of course lowered) was only THREE FUCKING
POUNDS AWAY this time. of course i gave up just as i give up
on everything. XX pounds. XX XX XX. like a heartbeat. XX, i
need it.

i sometimes stare at those pictures, those bony pictures
of girls who made it as far as they wanted. i think, *it looks
so painful*. then i say, *it's not*. being XX was nothing just
like being XX would be nothing except a little more tiring,
exhausting, floating, whatever.

the further down the weight goes the more obsessive the
thoughts become. when i dropped below XX and wanted to get
to XX, it was mostly so i could allow myself to eat and know
that i would gain weight and get to XX again without fear. but
then getting to XX became so much that i had to do it, had to
had to had to do it do it please because i said.

marya hornbacher was right, how when you're better you
keep this talisman of your eating disorder. you know it's there,
somewhere, the bones are still buried.

it's why i won't just tie a knot in it and be done.

i'm not really better. just the shell of better. just the idea of better. the charade.

but i mean, it works out, right? everybody sees me healthy and i say, "yeah, okay" and i don't give in to my dark desires of the destructive.

whatever.

XxLUCYS_LIGHT_DREAMxX   [entries | archive | friends | userinfo]

cw/gw in bio

[userinfo | livejournal userinfo]
[archive | journal archive   ]

regret   [May 24, 2005 | 04:32 am]

regret

regret

regress.

XxLUCYS_LIGHT_DREAMxX   [entries | archive | friends | userinfo]

cw/gw in bio

[userinfo | livejournal userinfo]
[archive | journal archive   ]

-   [May 25, 2005 | 06:08 pm]

i don't believe in the eating disorder speaking for you, thinking
for you, or taking over your brain.

it's all you.

yes, you are really that fucking crazy.

[comments disabled for this post]

XxLUCYS_LIGHT_DREAMxX   [entries | archive | friends | userinfo]

cw/gw in bio

[userinfo | livejournal userinfo]
[archive | journal archive   ]

architecture   [May 28, 2005 | 11:23 pm]

you told me you see metropolitan and suburban decay as
wasted potential, depressing, unused, left to rot in its ruins

my name is weakness and my name is torture my name is
rome and fuck everything you know, because dying a slow
passionate death is something i long for

maybe someday they'll find me, greyed, hardened, my stone
half standing against the sun and rain

i said my name is rome and i live for my ruins

[current music | nothingface - breathe out]
[1 comment | post comment]

XxLUCYS_LIGHT_DREAMxX   [entries | archive | friends | userinfo]

cw/gw in bio

[userinfo | livejournal userinfo]
[archive | journal archive   ]

-   [May 29, 2005 | 02:45 am]

last night repeating the mantra
'don't think. only sleep.'
only to wake up and find it worked; a first,

maybe it is not me that belongs in this body. maybe i belong
in a different body, a body with someone else's mind. there
are people who, all the time, are born in the wrong body. i was
born the wrong person, too.

this is my identity crisis. i feel like a black hole, its cliche,
i know. but how do black holes translate into human social
order? i don't know what i'm supposed to be on the outside

XxXDvSxBaBeXxX (1:37:47 AM): i've been wanting donuts and pizza.
hungerbound (1:37:48 AM): MMmmmm
lucifer_dramamine (1:37:50 AM): Mmmm.
hungerbound (1:37:52 AM): OH MY GOD PIZZA
lucifer_dramamine (1:37:54 AM): LOL
XxXDvSxBaBeXxX (1:37:58 AM): i love papa johns.
hungerbound (1:38:03 AM): like... a heartattack meat pizza
XxXDvSxBaBeXxX (1:38:05 AM): i want a HUGE cheese.. with x-cheese pizza. -sigh-
lucifer_dramamine (1:38:05 AM): I want a thin crust pepperoni.
hungerbound (1:38:13 AM): lol
hungerbound (1:38:24 AM): thin crust, extra cheese, extra pepp?
XxXDvSxBaBeXxX (1:38:25 AM): thin crust stuff is soo gooood.
hungerbound (1:38:25 AM): most def
lucifer_dramamine (1:38:39 AM): I want a tofu dog.
XxXDvSxBaBeXxX (1:38:43 AM): ew. never had one.
lucifer_dramamine (1:38:45 AM): Or tofu.. cooked.
hungerbound (1:38:50 AM): i love fried tofu
XxXDvSxBaBeXxX (1:38:50 AM): never had tofu period.
XxXDvSxBaBeXxX (1:38:57 AM): .. oO.. i want a funnel cake.
lucifer_dramamine (1:38:58 AM): It's actually good. Tofu tastes like whatever you cook it with :o)
hungerbound (1:38:59 AM): its good
XxXDvSxBaBeXxX (1:39:01 AM): with a lot of powdered sugar.
lucifer_dramamine (1:39:04 AM): MMM. FUNNEL CAKE.
hungerbound (1:39:05 AM): funnel :<
XxXDvSxBaBeXxX (1:39:10 AM): ohh... so ew.. is it like.. waxy? lol
lucifer_dramamine (1:39:18 AM): Tofu?
hungerbound (1:39:23 AM): waxy?
XxXDvSxBaBeXxX (1:39:25 AM): and movie theatre popcorn.. with extra butter. -sigh-.
hungerbound (1:39:26 AM): its spongey
XxXDvSxBaBeXxX (1:39:27 AM): ya.. like..

XxXDvSxBaBeXxX (1:39:30 AM): EW.. spongey!?
hungerbound (1:39:37 AM): well its not like... chewing on a sponge
XxXDvSxBaBeXxX (1:39:42 AM): 0_0
lucifer_dramamine (1:39:46 AM): Yeah.. it's kinda jello when its not cooked/spongey. But not gross spongey.
hungerbound (1:39:54 AM): its just kinda ... chewy
hungerbound (1:39:56 AM): its good
XxXDvSxBaBeXxX (1:39:57 AM): ohh..
XxXDvSxBaBeXxX (1:39:57 AM): hm.
hungerbound (1:39:59 AM): try some sometime
XxXDvSxBaBeXxX (1:40:06 AM): i might have to. but someone else will have to buy it first.

XxLUCYS_LIGHT_DREAMxX   [entries | archive | friends | userinfo]

cw/gw in bio

[userinfo | livejournal userinfo]
[archive | journal archive   ]

-   [May 30, 2005 | 01:01 am]

i forgot to say i graduated and it was whatever. i locked myself
in my basement for two weeks, writing/painting/listening
to music/railing adderall. mike and i texted on and off. he
introduced me to this band called tool. which incidentally i've
already been listening to for a while without knowing who
they were. they had this new album come out called *10,000
days*. mike was explaining to me what math rock is, that
some of their songs are based on the fibonacci sequence...
the only math i'm used to doing is what i put in my body, but
i guess i can dig looking at numbers as a kind of language of
life or energy that somehow speaks to a deeper sense of self.
especially with music, which is an experience that, for me,
feels outside of material experience, outside of my body. one
reason i love adderal so much... it puts me out of it, out of
my body, i don't have to think about it because the body just
functions so cleanly on it, and then i can just live inside my
mind. away from my meat suit. outside of it.

but now i've run out. and i don't want to see jenny again and
tell her what i've been doing. she'll be pissed. i've obviously
lost weight. and now i am having a hard time understanding
reality.

i don't get it anymore. isn't there supposed to be some point
you get to where you can say "there." and be done with the
misery? be done with the loneliness?

i hate this life

what is the point anymore?

and what is the right way to deal effectively with being alive?
why is it that escapism is so wrong?

but any way to deal is a form of escapism?

and what about love? why is it undefinable? why can't i just
accept it? why can't i find it? why can't i settle on one feeling
and just have it make sense?

i can't see jenny because i told her i was going to try to be normal. so i eat an apple. then i eat a chocolate. then i eat a rice crispy square.

and then i eat a six inch sub, sushi, chips and dip, ice cream. i run out of room and puke my guts out, drink water, take a rolaids, eat four pop tarts, puke, make popcorn covered in melted cheese, take laxatives, eat popcorn, eat more ice cream, then some macaroni, then just hunks of cheese….

my hands smell like bile. there is vomit in my hair.

i will have Total cereal for lunch, an apple for dinner, or vice versa, baby carrots and fat free yogurt as a snack. i can legitimately stick to this plan.

i need to go buy Bronkaid and caffeine pills.

i feel sick to my stomach.

i am not allowed to step on a scale.

i feel more sad at this point. that this is a necessary step to take. that time moves too slowly. that ultimately i know i will be moving alone through this world.

Comment By: **ms_molko**
2005-05-30 1:44 am (UTC) Select: Edit Delete Screen
Freeze Track This
(19.168.255.84)

i am so sorry baby. i'll move through with you.

XxLUCYS_LIGHT_DREAMxX   [entries | archive | friends | userinfo]

cw/gw in bio

[userinfo | livejournal userinfo]
[archive | journal archive   ]

-   [May 30, 2005 | 12:16 pm]

do you think it is possible for my thighs to get bigger over the
course of 12 hours

<thighs1.jpg>
<thighs2.jpg>
<backrib.jpg>
<stupidface.jpg>

ugh.

ugh ugh ugh

i can feel it.

i need my disorder.

today i weighed in at XX lbs.

but no more weighing.

Comment By: **hungerbound**
2005-05-30 12:34 pm (UTC) Select: Edit   Delete   Screen
Freeze   Track This
(76.188.116.102)

*"Pain is a food. A food that is essential to the growth of one's
soul."*

*I read that in the foreword of this comic, JTHM. Have you read
it?*

Maybe your soul is just really hungry, babe.

~~monday- 275 cals~~
~~tuesday - 1340 cals :(~~
wednesday- fast 6am-6am
thursday- fast 6am-6am
friday- 200 cals
saturday- 100 cals
sunday- 200 cals
monday- 100 cals

XxLUCYS_LIGHT_DREAMxX   [entries | archive | friends | userinfo]

cw/gw in bio

[userinfo | livejournal userinfo]
[archive | journal archive   ]

-   [June 3, 2005 | 10:22 pm]

tonight is another techno night at club Vue, but since i'm
"sick" i didn't go. i am on too many painkillers to really give
a damn, i guess. i wanted to go in case mike would be there
but i can't. part of me is afraid to see him. i'm afraid he is
going to make me want to feel all these human, girly things.
i hate that, i hate feeling like a girl. feeling emotional, i hate
wondering why he hasn't called, why i give a damn, why i
should even care if anything could ever happen. it's not like
we stopped talking on bad terms, we just haven't come in
contact in over a month.

god i really want to see him. i don't want to be human.

i guess it's different because you can't tie yourself up. you can
still bang your wrists against metal bars and hope they bruise,
but it just doesn't have the same effect.

brian keeps texting me and all it does is make me long for
someone. make me long for the days when i had someone to
call anytime and hold me anytime and someone i had to fight
with. we are both two different people now, though, i know
nothing would ever come of us again. i am just so lonely.

i am fighting it. one part of me says, i don't need it. i don't
need love. i don't need friendship. i don't need anything. and
then i keep thinking, *i have feelings, too! i'm human! I NEED
TO BE LOVED. please be fair to my heart.*

[current music | denial - sevendust]
[4 comments | post comment]

xylitoljen (10:23:31 PM): L... that counselor thing. Which is pretty obvious you know and if you don't, well, I'm confessing. I'm sorry. It was before I had gotten your email and I didn't know what to do. I was confused and scared for you until you consoled me with the email. I tried to convince her otherwise today, but I failed. I didn't want to cause you trouble. And I apologize. You've just never freaked me out so much before.
lucifer_dramamine (10:25:57 PM): It's okay.. I kind of figured it was. Lol. Amanda was like, "who turned you in?" And I actually wanted to let you know that I dont actually think of it as you "turning me in." It's okay to be worried and freaked out and stuff.. cause I understand. But I just want to let you know that if I do find this getting too serious for me, I'm going to let you know. If I start thinking I need help, I'm going to tell you.
xylitoljen (10:27:26 PM): All right. I understand that now. Sorry I didn't have more faith in you before. I was researching it and it just scared the shit out of me. I don't think I've ever been so panicked. Feel special, you make me irrational.

XxLUCYS_LIGHT_DREAMxX   [entries | archive | friends | userinfo]

cw/gw in bio

[userinfo | livejournal userinfo]
[archive | journal archive   ]

the story so far   [June 8, 2005 | 03:45 pm]

2005 #~~R~~→

CHICKS

~~Jamie~~ Thinkler	-	aquarius
~~Jessica~~	-	Virgo
Mikaela ~~█████~~	-	cancer
Vanessa H~~████~~	-	Aries
Laura ~~█████~~	-	Virgo

ILLOGICAL REASONS

Suffering is necessary for growth. Comfort is the opposite of suffering. Comfort is health. Therefore health is not suffering and I am not growing.

Pain is the food of the soul

I feel like cutting so bad. But I'm supposed to be in a better place.

Every time I stare at my wrists I feel like slashing them up.

Why? Where does this come from?

I don't want to die. I have hopes and dreams.

2500 - tuition
500 × 5mos = 2500 rent etc

$5000 for 5mos.

I leave craters
everywhere I go.

I bleed complexity.

My excess is evident in
everything.

My clothing choices,
my bed, my walls.
Everything.

My New Year's Resolution
is to become a
~~minimalist~~
GAH

is to become a

minimalist.

the joy

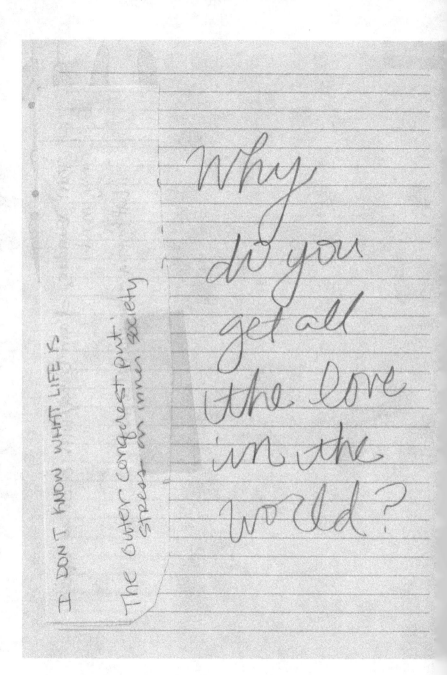

Why do you get all the love in the world?

I DON'T KNOW WHAT LIFE IS

The outer conquest put a spree on inner society

atiently WAITING
FOR THE DEATH OF GOD.

The impact I
have made
thus far is
merely a dent
in the earth

I will dig a
hole to china

I can't fucking eat right.
I never will. It's either too much
or not enough.

My fucking stomach hurts now
and all I wanna do is sleep
but I'm going to go hang out with
Misha.

BREAKFAST
2/40

total.

2 5   I stop

pros of recovering
- healthy hair
- no dry skin
- no hurting teeth (neutral)
- being warm
- energy to be social
- not being seen as crazy
- NO binge eating
- good (ish) body to others standards
- I am always living up to an "other"
- SEX DRIVE
- no more calculating calories

CONS of RECOVERING
(AKA pros of my disorder)
- being fat (thinness...)
- clothes don't fit (ARGH)
- feelings of inadequacy
- BEING FAT
- BEING FAT
- BEING FAT
- BEING FUCKING FAT
- having no other outlets

What steps do I need to take to get better?
• TO continue eating even when I am angry at myself

I feel like ~~HURTING~~ exploring the mind's capacity to affect the body

WORK IT. NO NO NO

I'm not eating today.

observable truth:
I am (XX) pounds.

Subjective truth:
I am a fat
piece of shit.

You have to
learn to let go...

of eating

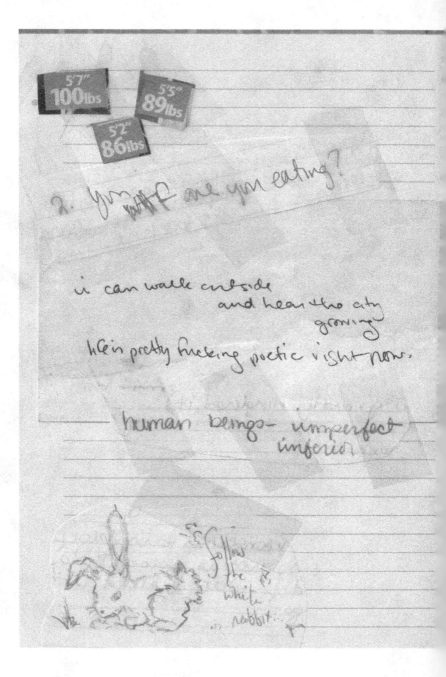

5'7"
100 lbs

5'5"
89 lbs

5'2"
86 lbs

2. ym wtf are you eating?

i can walk outside
          and hear the city
                    growing

life is pretty fucking poetic right now.

— human beings — imperfect
                    inferior

follow
the
white
... rabbit...

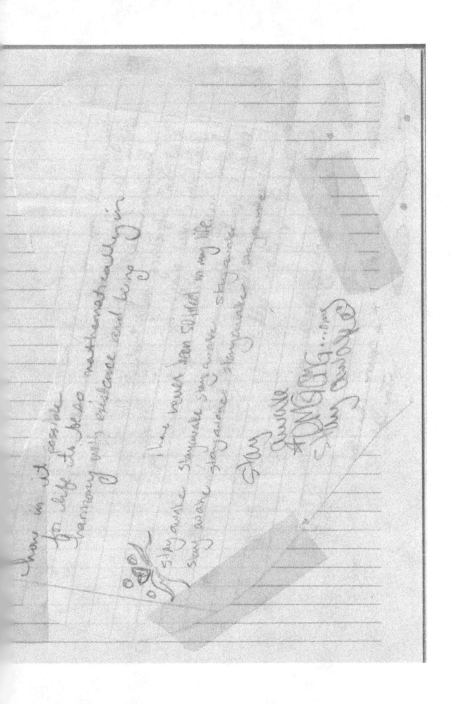

Since where I can't see it.

Health is so important. — I always find better outlets when I'm not starving myself.

By the way, yesterday I got a kitty ~~named~~ named his Frederich Nietzsch 🙂 but I call her Nie-nie (nee, nee) or stinky

Sunday (1 legume)

(11 grains)	(3 fruit)	(2 milk)	(4 veg)	(1 legume)	(1 fat)
cereal¹	70		— milk	90³	
1/4 c milk¹			2 sl bread	90 —	
mango¹	227		butter	50	
gran. bar²	90 → 317		jam	50~³	
ka_ spinach	33		sugar	120	
1s(?)³			(8 tsp!)		
oli_ o_	50 → 45		1 rice cake	50	
app_ ²	90 → 60³				
soy? ~3	85		→ total = ~~1450~~ =		
1s(bread)	45			1500	
cream cheese²	15	cut			
_ 6	120	down on			
cra_ ⁸	1160	sugar.			
	23 servings.				

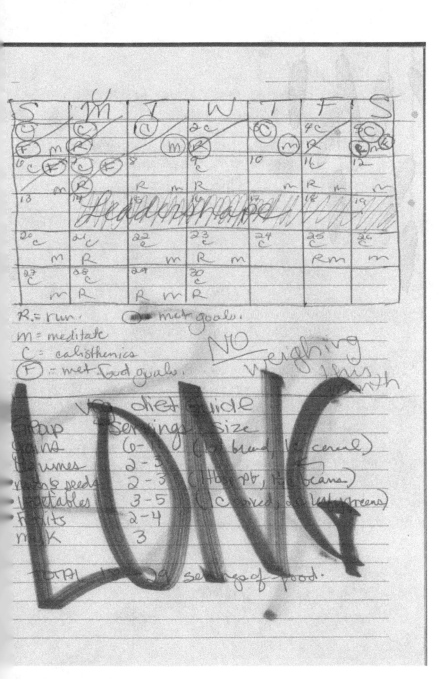

S	M	T	W	T	F	S
(C) (F) m	(C) (R)	(1)	2c	(C)	4c (R)	(C) (R)m (K)
6 c (F)	(C) (F)	8	9 c	10	11 c	12
m	(R)	R m R	16	17	m R m	19 m
13	14	Headache			18	
20 c m	21 c R	22 c	23 c m R m	24 c	25 c R m	26 c m
27 c m R	28 c R m R	29 c	30 c			

R = run.   (C) = met goals.
m = meditate
C = calisthenics
(F) = met food goals.   NO weighing this month

veg diet guide

Group	Servings	Size
grains	6-11	(1 sl bread, 1/2c cereal)
legumes	2-3	
nuts & seeds	2-3	(1tbsp pb, 1/2c beans)
vegetables	3-5	(1c cooked, 2c lettuce/greens)
fruits	2-4	
milk	3	

TOTAL = 19 servings of food.

monday.
I want to try organizing my diet through suggested intake.

LIST TYPE & caloric content.

GRAINS	Legume	nuts	vegetable
granola bar 90	1 tbsp PB 95	1 tbsp PB 95	
cereal 110	1 tbsp PB 95	1 tbsp PB 95	
cereal 110			
english muff 120	680		
eng. muffin 120	20		

550   1260

This is the guideline for a _____

170
4
0

healthy diet.

FRUIT	MILK	Total	OILS	sugar
apple 70	yogurt 40 cal		4 tbsp butter 200c	4 cookies
banana 105	milk 90			170·4 = 680c
	milk 90			

Still binging...

YOU

175, 220 = 2205

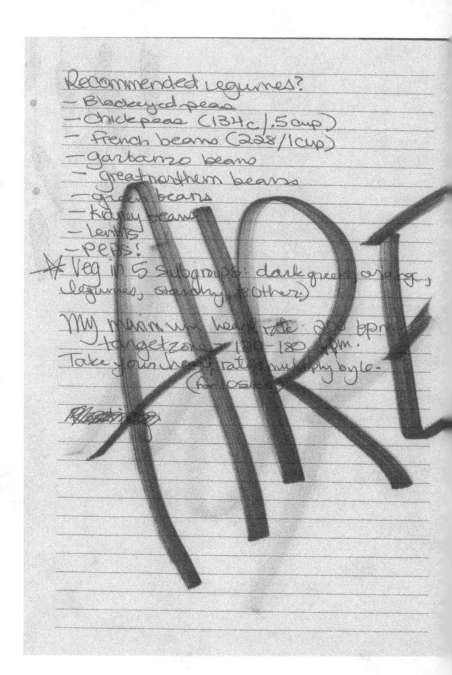

Recommended Legumes?
- Blackeyed peas
- Chickpeas (13¼c/.5 cup)
- French beans (228/1cup)
- garbanzo beans
- greatnorthern beans
- green beans
- kidney beans
- lentils
- peas!

※ Veg in 5 subgroups: dark green, orange, legumes, starchy, & Other.)

My maximum heart rate: 200 bpm
  target zone = 130-180 bpm.
Take your heart rate, multiply by 6-
       (for 10sec)

Tuesday

8 4

grains	legume	nuts	veg
eng muf	1 tb PB		salad
120	95		25
eng muf	1 tb PB		soup
120	95		42
1st bread	1 tb PB		soup
45	95		42
1st bread	1 tb PB		
	95		
bun	1 tb PB		
70	9.5		
	168		

fruit	milk	oil	
apple	yogurt	3 tbsp	TAL:
70	40	150	24
	milk		110
	40		
	5		1234
	1 2 3 4		

crackers	80	
pf	80	
englishmuffin	120	2049
butter	50	
pf	80	
cereal	70	tapering
milk	90	off
sugar	45	

Wednesday

Okay this isn't working.

Today my goals are:
3-5 servings veg
2 servings dairy
4 servings legumes
2-4 fruit serving
6 grain

eat these
before
anything else.
1600 calories
also to go jogging for 30 minutes
do my calisthenics
call Aunt Able Waters for appt

PLAN

Breakfast
- yogurt (1 dairy)
Lunch
- orange (1 fruit)
Snack
- apple (1 fruit)
Dinner
- Soup B Salad (3 veg)
Snack
- rice crackers (?)
- granola bar (1g)
- extra fruit cup? (3 fruit)
Supper
- Potato soup! (4 veg)
Snack
- Some kind of beans? (1-2 legume)

GRAINS	VEG
• rice 62	• salad
• bread	• salad
	25
• granola	• spinach
90	13
• cereal	•
70	
• cereal	•
105	
• rice cake	////
50	////

2/1
8 30
105
70
30
90
15
133

My binging seems to be tapering off...
Which is good. Binging makes me
upset. I want to do colonics to clean
me out and also because I'll be
"washing away" the "old me" so to
speak. ~~I know it seems gross but~~
~~my belly is full and it disgusts me~~
~~I wish I could dress like a boy~~
~~like a skinny androgynous boy.~~

FRUIT		LEGUME		DAIRY		OILS	
apple		beans		yogurt			30
	70				40		10
orange		proteins		milk			20
	40				90		20
		soybean		cream			70
					19		
							80

                                              760
+ running 30 mins   70
                                              830

1293 total

Rotten peach core of
my heart searches
for belonging but
finds a place to stand
                    instead.

AS
LONG

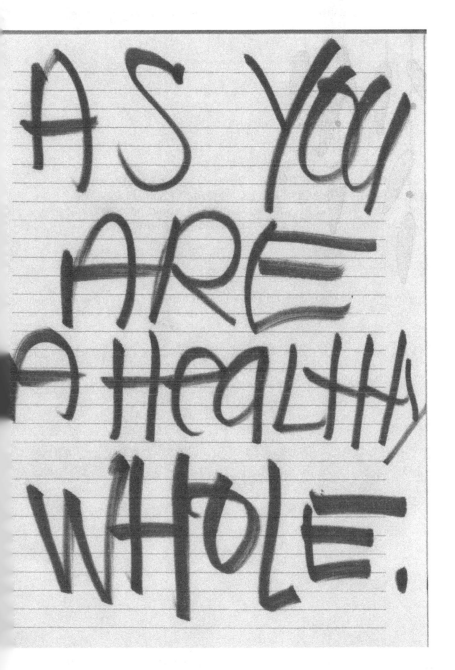

XxLUCYS_LIGHT_DREAMxX   [entries | archive | friends | userinfo]

cw/gw in bio

[userinfo | livejournal userinfo]
[archive | journal archive   ]

:([June 9, 2005 | 11:14 am]

of course my head swirls with mike...

this not talking/not calling

i keep thinking about the last time we saw each other, when
he came to my house so we could switch back shirts. i told
him to call me and he said he would— i would hate to think
that he would honestly say that without the intention to.

XxLUCYS_LIGHT_DREAMxX   [entries | archive | friends | userinfo]

cw/gw in bio

[userinfo | livejournal userinfo]
[archive | journal archive   ]

-   [June 9, 2005 | 09:15 pm]

i know hurting yourself is bad. i just keep thinking about it, again, the glass, something sharp against my thigh. blood. an easy way to repent for my fleshy orgy of food.

when i purge, i imagine mike's hands, the salty press of his fingers on my tongue reaching back, the sick curiosity on his face saying *how much can she take?*

~~monday- 900 cals~~
~~tuesday - 800 cals~~
~~wednesday- 375 cals~~
~~thursday- 680 cals~~
~~friday- 450 cals~~
saturday- 100 cals
sunday- 250 cals
monday- 100 cals

lucifer_dramamine (1:40:20 AM): lol
hungerbound (1:40:25 AM): haha
lucifer_dramamine (1:40:40 AM): mmmm.. popcorn.
XxXDvSxBaBeXxX (1:40:51 AM): i'm cheap.. and don't wanna waste money if i don't like it.
hungerbound (1:40:55 AM): some chick cooked popcorn in the hall
hungerbound (1:40:57 AM): i went NUTS
lucifer_dramamine (1:41:01 AM): I really want to eat something. I'm going to dream about what I should have for breakfast.
hungerbound (1:41:02 AM): i just stood there and inhaled for a while
XxXDvSxBaBeXxX (1:41:04 AM): haha aww
XxXDvSxBaBeXxX (1:41:09 AM): OMFG BREAKFAST.
lucifer_dramamine (1:41:12 AM): WHAT SHOULD I HAVE FOR BREAKFAST. that's low calorie :o(
hungerbound (1:41:14 AM): dude i was just thinking the same thing
XxXDvSxBaBeXxX (1:41:20 AM): ... -southern comes out-
hungerbound (1:41:25 AM): i was like... "OOOH SAUSAGE AND PANCAKES (but what will i really have)"
XxXDvSxBaBeXxX (1:41:30 AM): i'd like some biscuits and chocolate...
lucifer_dramamine (1:41:30 AM): Yeah, me too XD
hungerbound (1:41:41 AM): it honestly makes me cry sometimes
lucifer_dramamine (1:41:41 AM): mmm..
hungerbound (1:41:45 AM): just like... how unfair it is
hungerbound (1:41:51 AM): even though i could technically go eat whatever i want
XxXDvSxBaBeXxX (1:41:52 AM): some pancakes.. some sausage.. and CRISPY BACON.. and grits.. and biscuits.. and eggs.. both kinds.
hungerbound (1:41:53 AM): i CAN'T

XxLUCYS_LIGHT_DREAMxX   [entries | archive | friends | userinfo]

cw/gw in bio

[userinfo | livejournal userinfo]
[archive | journal archive   ]

-                              [June 11, 2005 | 07:07 pm]

i was a mold of mud
with an iron cast around
my insides festered and
waiting

there was a
rod in your hand
a hammer in the other

you couldn't
take it for what it was

and jagged edges stop the
teeth from touching

i was never different
i have never changed
i will always
be the fucking
same

hungerbound (10:23:15 PM): help, I'm fucking up
lucifer_dramamine (10:23:31 PM): look at trigger pics
hungerbound (10:23:15 PM): it's not helping.
lucifer_dramamine (10:23:31 PM):i'll hit you with the satanic statements
hungerbound (10:23:31 PM): okay
lucifer_dramamine (10:23:31 PM): taste is a temporary desire. When you satisfy it, it only grows. Thin is a constant desire. When you satisfy it, it only shrinks
lucifer_dramamine (10:23:31 PM): thin is a skill
lucifer_dramamine (10:23:31 PM): an imperfect body reflects an imperfect person
lucifer_dramamine (10:27:26 PM): pain is only as real as you allow it to be
lucifer_dramamine (10:27:26 PM): calories can't make you happy
lucifer_dramamine (10:27:26 PM): if you want food, look in the mirror at your thighs (even though I love yours ^-^;)
lucifer_dramamine (10:27:26 PM): hearts live by being wounded
lucifer_dramamine (10:27:26 PM): there can be no reality to the things you want unless you have structure in your mind first

the word is control

if you can dream it, you can do it

XxLUCYS_LIGHT_DREAMxX   [entries | archive | friends | userinfo]

cw/gw in bio

[userinfo | livejournal userinfo]
[archive | journal archive   ]

thunder night   [June 13, 2005 | 07:46 pm]

the thickness in my stomach
has dispersed over my thighs,
layers, over my hipbones, in my
forearms; there she will sit. she waits. weight
waits for the flurries and purple dotted skin.
it is almost here. i want to stand, arms outstretched
to fingers, feet taking root in my front yard.
want to grow branches, leaves, gaunt
decay of summer shrubs.
goodbye, green world.

cell phones ring and all i see are words
from boys with dicks as big as their egos.
they want me to come out and play.
i'm never sure why. i want to be
sequoia. but wood only stays hard
for so long. there is nothing here
for you, i want to say. stay wary and shy away
from the bright light.

XxLUCYS_LIGHT_DREAMxX   [entries | archive | friends | userinfo]

cw/gw in bio

[userinfo | livejournal userinfo]
[archive | journal archive   ]

-
                                                            [June 15, 2005 | 09:03 pm]

today i sat on my ass in front of the computer, and my mom
came up to me and handed me a National Enquirer. she says,
"i bought this for you, i figured you'd like it because of the
subject matter."

the cover reads: *WASTING AWAY. Stars risking their lives to
be thin!*

~~thursday- 2430 cals~~
~~friday- 1780 cals~~
saturday- 600 cals
sunday- 800 cals
monday- 600 cals
tuesday- 400 cals
wednesday- 200 cals
thursday- 1200 cals

XxLUCYS_LIGHT_DREAMxX   [entries | archive | friends | userinfo]

cw/gw in bio

[userinfo | livejournal userinfo]
[archive | journal archive   ]

-   [June 17, 2005 | 03:09 am]

a succession of bad days leads to the innate urge to self
destruct. love is back from it's summer vacation. that is what
i'm good at. you have to understand, i am going to hurt myself
no matter what. i like it that way. i look better on my knees,
crying.

everything i fight against, the stereotype, whatever. neurotic
and binge eating, leaving the pantry doors open. i can't
stop eating, and it's not even about being fat anymore.
understandably, it's still about losing weight. i just hate my
being. my body is representative of that. i would like to
slowly, but surely, cut away until there is no more. could you
imagine that? a razor blade and piece by piece, i drop off into
the bottom of the tub. all that red painting me real. i'm not
even a REAL eating disordered person. i'm a phony. a crash
dieter. a fake. NOT REAL. i put on a charade of self hate, but it
DOESN'T SHOW. so obviously i'm just not trying hard enough.

this self-denial is almost erotic. if only i weren't doing it to
myself.

[current music | mudvayne - -1]
[8 comments | post comment]

XxLUCYS_LIGHT_DREAMxX   [entries | archive | friends | userinfo]

cw/gw in bio

[userinfo | livejournal userinfo]
[archive | journal archive   ]

-   [June 17, 2005 | 04:01 am]

today my mom said to me, "i know you miss Jenny a lot, but you know you can talk to me about anything, okay?" which made me feel good but i won't talk to her because yeah. "hey mom i'm throwing up my food and starving myself because i hate myself and want to die!" isn't the way i want to tell her i love her and thanks for being there.

XxLUCYS_LIGHT_DREAMxX   [entries | archive | friends | userinfo]

cw/gw in bio

[userinfo | livejournal userinfo]
[archive | journal archive   ]

-   [June 17, 2005 | 05:45 am]

why can't i Maintain Composure? beth said it, at work. you
have to Maintain Composure. i said it to myself. Control
Yourself, you fucking female. i mean i know i'm at home losing
it this time... so it's okay to lose it, my room is a safe place.

except it's not. mom also told me to go watch a movie to
numb my mind off of the problems. that doesn't help. ignoring
the problems (worries about the future, my incompetence) will
not make them go away. i starve for that anyway.

XxLUCYS_LIGHT_DREAMxX   [entries | archive | friends | userinfo]

cw/gw in bio

[userinfo | livejournal userinfo]
[archive | journal archive   ]

-   [June 18, 2005 | 04:35 pm]

i'm spiraling down
circling
smaller

i'm not even afraid anymore

~~thursday- 2430 cals~~
~~friday- 1780 cals~~
~~saturday- 600 cals~~
~~sunday- 3845 cals :(~~
monday- 600 cals
tuesday- 400 cals
wednesday- 200 cals
thursday- 1200 cals

-   [June 19, 2005 | 11:32 am]

i think that ice cream in my fridge was like two or three years old. it tasted sour but i ate it anyway.

i wake up and lay in bed for 30 minutes. i have to set a couple of different alarms so i actually get up on days like this. every day it seems i keep sleeping deeper, but it's just more and more restless. i get phone calls at 4am from drunken boys i am too fat for, too bruised for, too cut up.

i wake up and i lay in bed and roll around. i fall onto the floor to put on pants and shoes and get my water bottle. i fill it with sugar free caffeine drink and exercise like a rat on a wheel for 45 minutes.

i space out, like making up for lost sleep. everything i can't be. i think about what i'm going to wear to work that day, if i even care; i tell myself this is going to be a good week; i swear up and down there'll be no more bingeing and purging; no more cycling; i have to calm down.

i, emotionally volatile.

i get off my little vermin wheel and grab a cup of coffee, count the calories in my teaspoon of creamer and drift to my shitty little room at the back of the trailer, with the window watching over the street that embodies all of my teenage years. i think to myself: i have to get out of here.

soon. soon beats through my head rhythmically like a drum freeing my insides (it is depressing that the only freedom i can feel right now is purging).

i sit at my computer hovering over my cup of coffee.

there are candy wrappers, diet soda cans, and sticky bowls left out from last night's horror. there are unanswered emails in my inbox because my brain is too dulled out from the rawness in my mouth and in my stomach. i swear i will make July count.

i will swallow the darkness.

instead of it swallowing me.

Comment By: **hungerbound**
2005-06-19 12:46 pm (UTC) Select: Edit Delete Screen
Freeze Track This
(76.188.116.102)

Envision a world free of fat people! Where TV advertisements
about lowering your cholesterol will no longer interrupt your
prime time viewing pleasure!

XxLUCYS_LIGHT_DREAMxX   [entries | archive | friends | userinfo]

cw/gw in bio

[userinfo | livejournal userinfo]
[archive | journal archive   ]

-   [June 20, 2005 | 08:45 am]

last night i dreamed someone took my teeth out of my head
and showed me the damage

the ones at the back were all black and rotten and soft

i can rinse my mouth out with water and feel spots in my
gums that burn

XxLUCYS_LIGHT_DREAMxX   [entries | archive | friends | userinfo]

cw/gw in bio

[userinfo | livejournal userinfo]
[archive | journal archive   ]

don't beat   [June 20, 2005 | 06:37 pm]

i want my skin scaledwith lockets securedwith small keys i
swallow downdream in which i was tin andhollow inside no
guts to fill medream: to be slit open scaredof this side of
human softflesh touch crumbleson my tongue i will never
learndream: hollow inside (go nuts and fill me)dream: will i
ever learn i will never learn this incomplete. a thingalways
missingdenial will not disappear youeven metal gives to
autumn rust

XxLUCYS_LIGHT_DREAMxX   [entries | archive | friends | userinfo]

cw/gw in bio

[userinfo | livejournal userinfo]
[archive | journal archive   ]

-   [June 21, 2005 | 02:01 am]

a while ago i wrote about the feeling of being trapped in a
body that was not mine.. comparing it to a gender crisis,
where boys feel they are trapped in girl bodies and vice versa.
i feel like i'm just the wrong person. i'm so out of my head
because i experience my body differently than most people
would experience theirs. i look down and it feels "wrong" in a
sense. it isn't meant to be there, it should be corrected, i can't
handle looking at it. i mentioned how i felt like a black hole
inside, but i don't know how black holes present themselves
in the human social order—like how should i be? how should a
person be, what rules can i follow just to get to a better place.
this is an identity crisis, or? maybe this quest for thinness
is that search for an identity. but then again i've hated the
feeling that i "am" my eating disorder. because i'm not. i don't
even feel like i'm allowed to call myself anorexic, even if by
diagnosable standards i am, i feel like the word itself brings
too much to mind that i don't fit. so it can't be that. maybe
this anguished journey is an expression of the disgust and
discontent i feel with being human or female or being in this
certain body. the idea of having a body outside of a mind is in
and of itself an insane thought to me and a bit disgusting. at
times i know the body is a vessel in which the mind lingers,
and i know the mind cannot exist without the body so this
can't really be an attempt to disengage the mind from the
body.. as doing so would destroy the mind in the process and
leave me with nothing, or at least something unknown and not
expressable in this world. another thing is that i get obsessed
with the idea of a body as a temple, and i know rationally that
what i'm doing is really degrading that temple but irrationally,
i feel like i can't disrespect that temple with things that are
unpure, like meat or processed things, so i only feed myself
fresh fruits or vegetables or things without additives or colors
or fillers.. but i do so to the point that it still degrades the
temple. which.. is a paradox. this whole thing is back and
forth. it's so weird. how can i know myself so well and still
have no idea who the hell i am?

[current music | hed(pe) - IFO]
[15 comments | post comment]

Comment By: **hungerbound**
2005-06-21 8:46 am (UTC) Select: Edit Delete Screen
Freeze Track This
(76.188.116.102)

*That REALLY made me think. It alarmed me, the way you
put it, because I can relate so well and I'd never been able
to connect like that before.I think of it like boot camp. Being
sent away to be disciplined and degraded and shaped-up and
hardened as fuck. No slacking off, no enjoyment, yet never,
EVER being "good enough." Never ever reaching a point where
there isn't still work to do. I don't deserve anything but the
bare minimum and that itself is only to get me to function
as something else, for someone else, and it is a mockery.
Think about it, it's humiliation. Like tossing a piece of bread
or gruel to a slave. It's humiliating and embarassing to be
given only that.I also understand what you mean about not
fitting anorexia despite being diagnosed as such. When I was
diagnosed anorexic, I was like, yeah, ok. But...I didn't really
have an "anorexic mind" at that point. I mean I was terrified
of food and irrational and had those thoughts, distorted
perception, but I was no longer JUST a robot... Like I had
more of an anorexic mind when I first started, when I was
ed-nos. As it became more and more about something much
other than just being thin,...it was like... I needed, I need a
higher purpose. I wasn't RIGHT. Something is off. There is this
whole, unexplored, mysterious beautiful world out there where
so many have trodden and had adventures and made impacts
and I'm not a part of it, I should be but I'm not becauuse I'm
not worth it. It's so fucking hard to explain and maybe it isn't
what you were takling about but just thought I'd try.Sorry htis
sucks so much. Sorry for the typos, too. There is a strip of
sinlight across my moniter (*sunlight) and I can't see a lot of
the things I am typing, but I know I have typos. Sorry.*

Comment By: **hungerbound**
2005-06-21 12:23 pm (UTC) Select: Edit Delete Screen
Freeze Track This
(76.188.116.102)

*except when I was lying on my bed and looking at my body
and feelingtrapped and detached, I thought maybe it is
something different than what i wrote here. there is this other
thing that happens. I assume youv'e read Wasted, lol. Well,
remember how she says that she always felt like she was an
octapus? lmao maybe she didn't say that. But that her body
was some organism or extremity dangling below her head...it
feels like that for me sometimes. Like I can't register it's me,
and I get anqry. I feel like it has its own hidden agenda, like
there is this underlying subconscious and malicious thought
it has. And I can move it and bend it but it is wrong, it's not
really me, it's like not even humoring me it's just... I don't
know.never mind, sorry.*

XxLUCYS_LIGHT_DREAMxX   [entries | archive | friends | userinfo]

cw/gw in bio

[userinfo | livejournal userinfo]
[archive | journal archive   ]

adderall   [June 21, 2005 | 10:15 pm]

i feel like a void. i mean inescapable
an emptiness you can't see

thickness with my feet sunk in
everything stops. i move so slow and
you speed things up

after years of this i've learned nothing about life
i know only of myself not as myself but
as some other distant species

gutter of a house bold against winter winds
soppy and dripping with muck
insects crept in

people live easy and unrelentless
here I am i am whining how hard it is to
survive with cold skin and aching bones

i feel disconnected like i'm so miserable
but i don't know where it comes from
and people ask me how i am, and i tell them

i'm doing really good
and it's not a lie
but then i still feel so lost

i don't think i feel my own emotions anymore
i just recognize them and articulate

[current music | this is love, this is murderous - bleeding through]
[4 comments | post comment]

cw/gw in bio

[userinfo | livejournal userinfo]
[archive | journal archive   ]

what can be said of me   [June 21, 2005 | 09:32 pm]

PLEASE

DEFINE I AND HUMAN EXISTENCE

HOW CAN I EXIST INSIDE THIS BODY
IF THIS I IS NOT WORTH THE FIGHT
TO KEEP THIS BODY OKAY

THIS VESSEL, THIS MASS OF HUMAN FLESH
IS INCONSISTENT WITH MY WISHES
THIS NOTHINGNESS INSIDE THE BODY
SCREAMS FOR RELEASE
THIS BODY
IS TOO
HEAVY

Comment By: **hungerbound**
2005-06-22 12:01 am (UTC) Select: Edit Delete Screen
Freeze Track This
(76.188.116.102)

*irony is the fact that eating disorders occur in societies where
food is most plentiful*

XxLUCYS_LIGHT_DREAMxX   [entries | archive | friends | userinfo]

cw/gw in bio

[userinfo | livejournal userinfo]
[archive | journal archive   ]

public entry   [June 22, 2005 | 12:05 am]

<thighsnlies.jpg>
<cigarette.jpg>
<nightpark.jpg>
<railme.jpg>

~~*~*

<mikeandlucyfuck.mov>

pain is there,
but the relationship
you have to it is
what will truly
determine where you stand
and how you fall

[current music | foolish pride - the deadlights]
[86 comments | post comment]

Comment By: **x2dJunglist**
2005-04-28 02:14 am (UTC) Select: Edit Delete Screen
Freeze Track This
(167.172.145.64)

*just…. take care of yourself, ok? it's how you do that worries
me. i know you're better than this. i don't get what happened
to you. that's why i'm worried. i have been, about your health,
forever… i wish i could turn you back to what you were. happy
and motivated and not a destroyer of everything. just … man
… i can't believe what's going on with you. even lately. you
look so damn sad. that's just weird to me. i wish you could be
happy like when we were together. and not be this stranger
with a thing for lust and destruction.*

<3 brian

thursday- 2430 cals
friday- 1780 cals
saturday- 600 cals
sunday- 3845 cals :(
monday- 90 cals
tuesday- 400 cals
wednesday- 200 cals
thursday- 4560 cals :(

XxLUCYS_LIGHT_DREAMxX   [entries | archive | friends | userinfo]

cw/gw in bio

[userinfo | livejournal userinfo]
[archive | journal archive   ]

\-

[June 23, 2005 | 10:03 pm]

i'm not allowed to open new boxes of food in my house.

no animal by-products. no milk, no eggs. no butter.

hungerbound (1:36:38 AM): my mom would buy those big jars of pickles
XxXDvSxBaBeXxX (1:36:42 AM): oOo yae.
XxXDvSxBaBeXxX (1:36:43 AM): yea*
hungerbound (1:36:47 AM): and i'd drink out all the vinegar before it was empty
XxXDvSxBaBeXxX (1:36:49 AM): oh god.. i LOVE vinegar stuff.
hungerbound (1:36:49 AM): she'd go nuts
hungerbound (1:36:52 AM): i LOVE VINEGAR
XxXDvSxBaBeXxX (1:36:57 AM): spicy stuff and vinegar stuff.. oh yes.
hungerbound (1:37:04 AM): dude... if you love vinegar you should really try the soy stuff
lucifer_dramamine (1:37:06 AM): I love spicy stuff <3.
XxXDvSxBaBeXxX (1:37:12 AM): haha me too. i'd get mad at myself b/c our pickles wouldn't be juicy. so i moderate.
hungerbound (1:37:12 AM): spicy D:
hungerbound (1:37:16 AM): my poor widdle tongue
XxXDvSxBaBeXxX (1:37:21 AM): hahaha
XxXDvSxBaBeXxX (1:37:25 AM): man.. soy sauce is just.. iono. it's so salty to me.
hungerbound (1:37:33 AM): that's why you mix it with vinegar
XxXDvSxBaBeXxX (1:37:37 AM): ohh that's right.
lucifer_dramamine (1:37:40 AM): I want a Krispy Kreme donut D:
hungerbound (1:37:42 AM): its SO GOOD
hungerbound (1:37:43 AM): me too
hungerbound (1:37:46 AM): and cinnamon toast crunch

body below me hang on tight   [June 24, 2005 | 03:34 pm]

my throat is sore from mike's fingers, and also mine, but mine is from filling it with junk, crying, unzipping skin.

my thighs, my thighs are huge okay? but what does it mean? what does it mean? huge thighs can't be symbolic of everything i've failed at, can it? can it simply mean it's too much for this world, i've spilled out of my allotted space, i don't want to cushion the boys that want my body beneath them. huge thighs mean everything in this underworld

is it sad? is it sad that i locked myself in a room and turned out the lights? i said, here's what i am now. what's there? no moving shadow? here the thighs are hidden the scars are hidden. if you stripped me down and drowned me what would you get?

what am i if no one wants me. nothing.

breathe, here, still, nothing.

what if i branded the words into my skin and felt all that it meant burn from me? in the darkness could you feel the warmth of my ether spilling quick and fast?

would i know what it means?

it's not me, can it be? brands do not burn into the soul and blood will not release my supposed inner beauty and i cannot find myself in textbook definitions, not type A not type B

and i feed into it, its sick and i feed it, the monster it grows pain fill me please

i wish i'd understand that i will always be the same Not Me underneath

[8 comments | post comment]

XxLUCYS_LIGHT_DREAMxX   [entries | archive | friends | userinfo]

cw/gw in bio

[userinfo | livejournal userinfo]
[archive | journal archive   ]

-   [June 26, 2005 | 12:15 pm]

last night mike texted me saying, "why do i like you so much?"

i woke up at 9am and i sat down at my kitchen table and let
myself eat two pieces of toast with peanut butter on them.
i drank four ounces of milk and stared out the window for a
while trying not to count anything.

i got depressed and went back to bed until about noon, after
finding out work was closed again due to a freak snowstorm,
this late in June, and was woken up again by my mom making
grilled cheese sandwiches. i ate one. one, not four.

text messages were exchanged between mike and i. he had
plans with his girlfriend but attempted to push them back so
we could hang out. he told me to wear snow clothes.

i have lived in colorado for ten fucking years and i am
astonished that i do not own snow clothes. i do have gloves
and a beanie and warm hoodies. but i've only owned a parka
once (that disappeared this year) and that's really it.

i dressed as warm as I could. jeans, three shirts, scarf etc.

he told me not to come up his street because cars were
getting stuck, so meeting him in the cul-de-sac next to this
park we were going to was a better idea. my car got stuck
halfway in the cul-de-sac before he got there. an SUV came
and pushed behind my car to get me out. i freak out about
people i don't know that try to help me with anything. but i
let him do it. it was nice. my car is still stuck. but mike and i
decided to play in the snow and worry about it later.

okay. can this get any more romantically pathetically
awesomely cute? we PLAYED IN THE SNOW. we ran around
and threw snow at each other and held hands and collapsed
in the snow. and kissed. i was SOAKED. it was so cold. i am
thankful to have had fuel in my body to keep me as warm as i
could. if I had been restricting or had not eaten, i don't know.
when you don't eat you get that cold feeling that comes from

inside that's impossible to warm up. i probably would have died ha. this is a start.

i'm trying to think more positively about the stuff i put in my body.

there was a point where i got hit in the face with snow! my make-up ran. i wanted to say something about it, complain, point out my mistakes so he couldn't do it silently. but i just ignored it. i wiped off my face and i wasn't horrifically ugly. a person i had to pretend to be strong for. he's so stable that if i'm not it might all fall apart. even with lopsided eyeliner smeared from the snow. i looked okay. after a while we went back to my car. he planned to run up to his house and get his snow shovel so we could dig my car out. while he was gone another kind stranger pulled my car out of the cul-de-sac backwards. mike came back and we headed off to find a parking lot so i could change out of my wet clothes and into some dry ones.

my gas light came on so we drove around to find a gas station, too. i filled up my car and we found a dark spot to park.

this is the part where i got horrified.

i have so many scars and cuts on my legs, deep ones. there are some from two weeks ago that haven't healed yet and there's no way to avoid not changing without being completely abnormal and pushing him away. which i didn't want to do. i unbuckled my belt and said, "okay. before i take off my pants can i tell you that my legs are mangled from being angry at the world." and he was like, "okay." and i took off my pants and hid in my hoodie. he put his hands on the bottoms of my thighs. the contact between him and me was too much. the heat of it. the thought of being cared for. he asked when i was mad at the world and i said, two weeks ago when i had texted him about it. when Jenny's cousin committed suicide. he said, "oh, okay. well, what did you do?"

i showed him. ... i showed him.

i feel like... i don't know. i was horrified but i needed to do it. if things end up getting heavier with us he would see it anyway. it's embarrassing. i have scars that form the word "grotesque" in my leg. i have big ones. another that says "coward." he ran his hands over them. i told him i felt crazy and he said, "you're not." he said he used to burn himself when he was younger and showed me his scars. for the first time in a long time i felt comfortable being vulnerable in the presence of someone i deemed threatening or intimidating.

unfolding. that's what i was doing.

i put on my dry pants and changed out of my shirt and he wrapped me up warmly for a couple minutes. we kissed, he put his hand against my neck. he said he wanted to keep me. i told him he should have postponed meeting up with his girlfriend (at 6:30) even though i knew he couldn't.

his hands searched for mine when we were walking, waiting to grab. he worried about my safety. it's so strange to me to feel *certain* that he likes me. like he's not just playing some kind of trick on me so he can one day push me in the dirt and laugh like it was all a joke. like he's not just playing a game, like he doesn't see me as a nameless doll with a wet mouth.

when we talk, it's sharing and that's intense! it's intense and it's so nice not to be so fucking closed up.

i gave him a gift, which i almost didn't because i felt so stupid. but i'm really glad i did. i bought him *Invisible Monsters* since he'd expressed an interest in reading more fiction. on the inside, i wrote "to mike; i hope you make the best mistakes."

something is different about today. that's the reason i'm telling you all this. usually when we part ways all i can do is think about how stupid i acted or all the bad things he could possibly think about me. i get really angry at myself and it sort of ruins everything and i just put him up on a pedestal in my head hoping i'll be forgiven by whoever. i didn't do that today. it's not even that i tried specifically not to, it just didn't happen. there's no pedestal, he's just this awesome guy and today was amazing. i was me and it was okay. i didn't down myself. i was just. there. existing and being.

cw/gw in bio

[userinfo | livejournal userinfo]
[archive | journal archive   ]

-   [June 27, 2005 | 10:05 am]

may my letters not reach tall to the heavens but stay put
beneath their margins.

today i woke up angry as i do every day. decided i didn't want
to eat breakfast, i feel immature and temper-tantrumish.
this little 12 year old girl in my head is stamping her feet and
grabbing her shoulders. no bones, it's thicker and when i rub
my spine i can't feel it anymore.

my skin is greasy because i'm bleeding.

it's funny because even though i feel fat, part of me revels in
the curves. when i was heavier last year i was overjoyed that
men found pleasure in it i guess. i'm afraid to wear real pants
though, i've just been wearing sweats and work clothes.

mike has said he likes me because i have a deeper
appreciation for the beauty of life than most girls he's met.
and various other things that are supposed to make me feel
good and that he likes me. i think this is supposed to instill
confidence inside of me, or reassurance that i'm not an
expendable person. which is one of my biggest fears, not just
in this situation but in general.

because i am expendable. i feel like a piece of pez. uh, forgive
the lameness of my analogy but it's true. one of many, little
fish in big sea etc etc blah blah. because as much as i feel
like an individual or someone that people will remember or
whatever, my fear of arrogance takes over and i realize i'm
not really unique matched against the plethora of other girls
in this situation, or people in general. everyone is their own
flower or snowflake or whatever unique crap because they all
unfold in their own ways. which then makes the uniqueness
of my own being insignificant. i don't mean this in a generally
detrimental way either, however that might be the underlying
feeling.

when brian and i stopped seeing each other, he told me i was
the most amazing person he's ever met... or something along

those lines. i never told you this, i elected to just stop the situation completely. he said me leaving "ruined his life" (i will never forget those words) and i told him the only reason i'm amazing to him is because he took the time to feel between the edges in a way he never did with nikita. when you put that energy into 'getting' to know someone.. into exploring the vastness of their being, it's easy to become overwhelmed by the great beauty they hold inside.

but everyone is like that. anyone can be amazing if only you take that time.

which is why i know i'm expendable and not as unique as i'd wish, for the simple fact that any energy put into someone can reveal that.

i still feel that "but it's different for _____ " because to ME (CAPS!) mike is not an expendable or replaceable person at all and neither are most of the people in my life. the people that are close to me. acquaintances, work associates etc, yes are their own special people but i don't know them, so. i don't know. that may be an asshole thing of me to say.

why am i pez-like and generic. and why are those that surround me snowflakes and flowers and beautiful fingerprints?

it's not that i need or want validation of being "a unique snowflake" but more, why is it not possible for me to perceive myself the way i perceive those around me? i can lay against the skin of another and worship the feel of it, but i can not touch my own body lest i be practicing my hygienic rituals, otherwise known as throwing up the things i eat and bleeding penance out of me. i can recognize the human faces of strangers and see them as neutral, i can see what i think is objective but when they see mine, why is it that my face is disfigured and has suddenly become very dirty and unacceptable? i can't believe another human can lay eyes on me and see me for what they think is something neutral, a face in a crowd of millions.

-   [June 29, 2005 | 02:24 am]

i think there's this heavy beauty to human existence that i can't touch even though i can experience it sometimes and remember that i experience it. but i feel so disconnected from everything like i'm not worth it.

and that's exactly the problem: not that i am not worth it, but that *i think* i am not worth it at all.

i think, i think—thinking is the problem.

i am not going to expect anyone else to see that i am worth it if i am not. if i set my standards for human behavior low, there is no room for disappointment.

i have been wary of this whole friendship i have with mike. as much as i let go and told him about myself, i still wanted to hold back because of everything that happened last time i let go and felt for someone.

this really sucks.

moving aside.

i'm really hurting because i want so badly to believe that i matter to someone. i've analyzed his behavior towards me and the obvious motivator is sex, because it always is. it's what humans do. but above and beyond that. i want someone to value my mind and being as much as they value my pussy. always, always, always. i found someone attractive, found out what they wanted, and gave it to them exactly as they wanted. because i, so graciously, live to fucking please. placebo.

every time the chance to score with me was closer, he was more interested. the only thing we lack is a place to that's not in a car or whatever.

he's been seemingly less interested in me. we're supposed to hang out tomorrow and he doesn't seem to care that much.

and tonight, he didn't really talk to me that much on the phone. we started texting later and he said, "well.. i'm going to go, i shouldn't really be texting anymore.. but you know what! some fucking girls played a prank on me last night" and i was like, "aw, what'd they do?" and he was like, "i have hickeys! fuckin a." so i texted him back like, "haha that's not exactly a prank ;) but i guess i'll talk to you later."

i mean i know he has a girlfriend... i don't get the point in telling me this. what fucking sucks is i wanted to tell myself this wasn't a game for once. FOR ONCE. i'm not playing but i'm pretty sure i am or was close to being played.

i got shut down. what reason does he have to tell me that? i can only guess he wants me to see he's more available than i care to know so i lose interest and stop pursuing, or he wants to make me jealous so i pursue him more adamantly? or he's testing me to see if i am the kind of person to get jealous? or he's trying to let me know he doesn't need me or my mouth anymore.

jenny said maybe it was a scapegoat, he needed to give me some explanation for them as though he owes me something despite this whole arrangement. still, my masochist mind is begging for any reason to push him away since all i want is to bring him closer.

circuits end where i begin   [June 29, 2005 | 08:01 am]

i made a new email address but i can't decide if i should allow myself to use it. people use email addresses as extensions of identity so that others will make certain assumptions about who that person is.

yeah, this is a lot more serious than it needs to be because it is JUST an email address but this kind of stuff is important to me. i also don't know if i'm in the right place right now to use it, because of what it means to me. i don't know if i deserve it because it's about progessively moving and i don't. i don't feel like i am moving forward at all. although i know i will be soon and maybe this would be a healthy reminder.

anyway, my new email address is eulerian.travels@gmail.com

euler was a profound mathematician, and in the 1700s he solved this problem called the Konigsberg Bridge problem. the question was whether or not one could pass over all seven bridges once and only once while ending up back at the same spot, which would be called a eulerian circuit. he found out that it was impossible. however, what i really like about this is this concept of the Eulerian path in which the path traverses ALL bridges one time, but does not have the same starting and ending point—meaning there isn't a cycle, there isn't any backpedaling. there is only progress.

in my mind, it represents the theoretical idea of escaping samsara—the cycle of death and rebirth. look, i know i'm a dumb bitch, but i've inexplicably become a math bitch. i am doing math and it's not nutritional math. it makes sense to me.

the reason i chose this name is because that right now i feel like a traveler who can see in what direction she needs to go. my goal is to take a path that takes me to each bridge, a bridge i can cross once and only once, like the rubicon, like many rubicons, thus progressing each time i do pass. the other thing is the relevance to the Eulerian circuit—how life *is* cyclical, no matter how you try to make it not.

does that make sense at all or is that completely bunk? i
would feel kinda dumb having an email address that doesn't
make sense. i also feel lame that doing something as simple
as changing an email address makes me feel the need to
completely explain why i have this email address, when most
people would just simply say that they felt like changing it and
left it at that.

should i use it?

XxLUCYS_LIGHT_DREAMxX   [entries | archive | friends | userinfo]

cw/gw in bio

[userinfo | livejournal userinfo]
[archive | journal archive   ]

grape pop   [June 30, 2005 | 12:21 am]

tonight i wore a shirt that i hadn't worn since i weighed under XXX. it used to be slightly loose on me and now it is very tight and you can see the roundness of my stomach. this is painful. i really think i'm going to start showering in the dark.

XxLUCYS_LIGHT_DREAMxX   [entries | archive | friends | userinfo]

cw/gw in bio

[userinfo | livejournal userinfo]
[archive | journal archive   ]

-   [July 1, 2005 | 3:23 am]

staring at my face in the mirror hurts because i've mapped all
the bad things that other people are going to judge me for.
like my bad skin. and my round cheeks and my hollowed out
speed-eyes. (and pleasepleaseplease. don't tell me, "oh, but
you are so gorgeous" because its subjective. what you see
is not the same as what i see. it doesn't help and gets me
further from my point) i don't understand when people who
"like" me look at me. i don't know what they see because
perspective is all subjective. it's so frustrating because. with
mike. i remember the first couple times i saw and talked to
him, he was like this divine piece of art. like his skin and hair
and the way his face was shaped. and his eyes and lips. they
all just fit together, like he was carved from marble. and with
me, i'm too soft and round and gelatinous. i don't know how
he sees me. i figure he sees me the way i do which is why
we don't talk as much anymore. which is sort of egocentric. i
know logically he is just busy with his band and his theories
and his girlfriend and his own life. but it's depressing because i
want to feel like i am worth the time it takes to write an email
or a text.

i am just doing the girl thing. that's another thing, all of this,
what i wanted to avoid. i don't want to be like this. it is just—
it's too typical.

[current music | chimaira - dead inside]
[2 comments | post comment]

~~friday- 600 cals~~
saturday- 1000 cals
sunday- 800 cals
monday- 1000 cals
tuesday- 400 cals
wednesday- 1000 cals
thursday- 200 cals
friday- 1000 cals

XxLUCYS_LIGHT_DREAMxX

[entries | archive | friends | userinfo]

cw/gw in bio

[userinfo | livejournal userinfo]
[archive | journal archive   ]

-

[July 2, 2005 | 9:05 am]

i am so present i forget what it's like to feel the past

XxLUCYS_LIGHT_DREAMxX   [entries | archive | friends | userinfo]

cw/gw in bio

[userinfo | livejournal userinfo]
[archive | journal archive   ]

each year the weight creeps up... i can't outrun this   [July 3, 2005 | 7:05 pm]

as old relationships become replaced by new i
find myself losing in a war of connections;
i fail at networking, i fail at seeing people,
i fail at seeing my community. i have now fallen
out. this is the vacuum. i am filling it with emptiness
forever and forever down.

the talisman is always lurking aux miroirs.

funny is this: as i've found the lost love of
my life i find myself threatened by previous
presences that have never done so before, at
least not with this much intensity. i must shrink—
fit myself into portable places to be carried always,
lest i be forgotten.

XxLUCYS_LIGHT_DREAMxX   [entries | archive | friends | userinfo]

cw/gw in bio

[userinfo | livejournal userinfo]
[archive | journal archive   ]

intrusive   [July 6, 2005 | 10:50 pm]

why do i even try to open up? sometimes i feel so lame for
wanting love so bad. sorry, i've been speedy today, finally
scored more adderal and now i can't stop thinking about mike.
for so long i've hated love and cursed it and kept myself from
feeling it. it makes me feel very pre-teen. to say that i want
mike, i want him to call me, i want him to give me attention
and to tell me he loves me. i want to go out for coffee with
him. to hold hands and walk in the rain, and play in the mud,
and do all the dumb things people do when they are in love.
i want to tell him these feelings but i'm so scared he doesn't
feel the same. at the same time, i question why i stay feeling
stuck on him when it's obvious he hasn't taken any time to
prioritize me. is he even thinking about me? why does he
sometimes not text back, but then if i don't, he'll never follow
up the way i do. is that utterly pathetic? low self-worth tricks?
i'm starting to question what i'm worth. if i am worth more, i
want reciprocation. does he fear me?

[current music | nonpoint - tribute]
[2 comments | post comment]

~~friday- 600 cals~~
~~saturday- 1000 cals~~
~~sunday- 800 cals~~
~~monday- 500 cals~~
~~tuesday- 400 cals~~
~~wednesday- 180 cals~~
~~thursday- 140 cals~~
friday- 90 cals

XxLUCYS_LIGHT_DREAMxX   [entries | archive | friends | userinfo]

cw/gw in bio

[userinfo | livejournal userinfo]
[archive | journal archive   ]

PARADOX OF MY LIFE: AS I SHRINK I GET BIGGER   [July 8, 2005 | 03:05 pm]

i am stuck at phase one

it has nothing to do with exterior consciousness

societal standard

familial pressure

its all me.

i hate myself.

i'm a fat piece of shit and i want to die.

better yet today people acknowledged my existence.

i can't get ahold of this, why i'm afraid: prefer the ground but
desire the figure. what i don't see is that reality is gestalt and
i'm both object, shadow and space around it.

[current music | on your way down - stabbing westward]
[8 comments | post comment]

XxLUCYS_LIGHT_DREAMxX   [entries | archive | friends | userinfo]

cw/gw in bio

[userinfo | livejournal userinfo]
[archive | journal archive   ]

-
[July 9, 2005 | 09:45 am]

the world is so depersonalized and i partake in it. i am trapped in mindsets that perpetuate the consumer culture. i don't want to anti-consume but i just want to fucking consume right. i am tired of the binge-starve cycle.

i just want to fucking eat normally. i want to run religiously. i fail at everything. i took two vicodin but my head still fucking hurts. i'm tired of wondering if mike is thinking of me. i'm wondering if being less of a construction to the "other" makes me less of a being.

i'm tired of dying to reach out to someone but staying in my shell. i'm tired of staring longingly at people holding hands, yearning for the feeling of human touch. i'm tired of touching my own skin trying to replicate that spark of warmth in another body. i'm tired of washing my face day and night only to find my acne won't go away and my image is still tainted.

i'm over being felt as a separate entity from reality. the separation is painful and agonizing.

i also need to just keep my fucking mouth shut. i feel like when people talk about a subject i'm interested in, i get too excited and share everything i know about it, and just come off as a stuck up bitch who thinks she knows everything. i just want to fucking share and i feel like thats rejected. i feel like people say i don't understand as a personal attack. i feel like everything i do is wrong. i feel like i'm too fucking defensive. i feel like curling up into a ball, swallowing pills till they burn holes through my stomach. when someone asks me how i'm doing, all i want to do is confess my troubles but i fucking CAN'T because no one deserves to have an emotional burden dumped on their shoulders, whether they care or not. no one should hear it. but it is so limiting to me. my intent is just to share. i want communion. i want human contact.

today i looked at trees and felt happy inside.

i started reading a bit more about the roots of suffering. i

just need to understand why we suffer, why people suffer.
in buddhism there is this thing called dependent origination,
which means that all suffering has a root cause. and to
stop the suffering you have to find the root cause and then,
idk, accept it, or try to understand it. i am starting to see
everything through this lens. i hate watching tv because i see
the hook and every minute that passes only causes to sink
me deeper into my self-hate. every product pounded into
my brain, every smiling face demonstrates to me the social
construction of beauty and i only feel less and less like a
beautiful person and more and more like a social deviance. i
deserve to be shot and ground up and fed to worms.

i am a fat piece of shit and that *only* means that i am not okay
with the space i take up.

i can only stand to tear at myself because i'm scared to reach
out. and i'm scared to reach up. potential is bright but my
eyes are sensitive.

my eyes feel blown out. my sleeping patterns are so fucked
up. one side of my face hurts from a tooth extraction and i'm
nauseated from this vicodin. i could just move to tibet and
smoke opium for the rest of my life.

i could, i could be the monk. forever distilling want into
nothingness. renouncing my personal and material belongings.
but i know the true path to freedom is not about being able to
starve and meditate for fourteen hours a day. it is not about
giving up what matters to me. it is about the fundamental
concepts of attachment and desire that must be given up.

i hate knowing this. knowing what is good for me and not
taking it. the importance of this-- "the main point is to develop
a state of mind that is not so consumed by attachment and
greed." (rita m. gross, elegance with just enough, from this
anthology i am reading called *hooked: buddhist writings on
greed, desire, and the urge to consume*). in buddhism this
word keeps coming up—"equanimity." i wasn't sure what it
meant. it sounds like being equal with all things that surround
you. when i see that word i think of two great scales attached
to my head, on either side of my body, each scale filled with
the equal amounts of happiness and sadness, sitting at perfect
level. and nothing disturbs the scales, not weight loss, not my
sense of self, not acne, not dick, not rejection, not mike.

i do *want* the middle path. a simple life that can cultivate this. its not necessary—but suffering is how i *wish* to live. its just easier and i am trying and failing and still getting caught in the hook.

i could just eat right and run religiously. i could make running a religion. i hate it. everything triggers me but i love it so much because it keeps me going on the wire. but no trigger lasts and i just stand to eat a bunch of shit that makes me hate myself. i would feel more confident if i had a girlfriend. i would feel less confident if i had a boyfriend, but i would feel less lonely. i'm just so fucking lonely. i have no validation but i can't seek it because it's vain and i am not supposed to live in construction of the other.

i'm so fucking depressed. i don't want pity, i want a hug. i want human contact. i want validation. i need love. i want to die. i want to live. i want to suffer. i want to feel. i want equanimity more than anything.

i want and i want and i want with hands grasping like a little wormbaby unaware of itself relation to the world surrounding it and i can't stand to just let myself be and come back to pieces collecting on the terms of natural movement or the structure of things.

[current music | one minute silence - south central]

[4 comments | post comment]

~~sunday- 650 cals~~
~~monday- 1400 cals~~
tuesday- 650 cals
thursday- 1000 cals
friday- 650 cals
saturday- 600 cals
sunday- 650 cals

cw/gw in bio

[userinfo | livejournal userinfo]
[archive | journal archive   ]

-   [July 11, 2005 | 11:23 pm]

i told jenny about how in psych class once, two girls did a
presentation on eating disorders and fucked it up. the teacher
and everyone proceeded to find proanorexia on lj and make
fun of it. i still despise that pro-ana is the poster child for
the typical eating disordered person. i am not like that, and
most of us aren't. i told jenny how i'd been nervous because
i was at a pretty low weight and had to go up after them. she
laughed, without thinking, and said, "no one noticed."

this isn't an attack against her or what she said by any means,
so don't interpret it that way. but to this day i will never forget
that.

no one noticed. do you know how fucking right she is. do
you know how long i will suffer this way, under the guise of
an overachieving student, how no one will know my secrets?
do you know how much effort and how much hard work i
would put into destroying myself, only to have no one notice?
sometimes, to me, this is so fucking triggering. because I was
never good enough before, and now for some reason i have
to be. don't take me as delusional yet, i still see the error in
my logic, okay? i understand that. i'm just pointing out the
thought patterns.

no one noticed.

[current music | mindless self indulgence - bitches]
[14 comments | post comment]

lucifer_dramamine (4:00:58 AM): I talked about you today
x2dJunglist (4:01:17 AM): really?
x2dJunglist (4:01:19 AM): to whom?
x2dJunglist (4:01:23 AM): about what?
lucifer_dramamine (4:01:13 AM): Yeah. To a co worker, my assistant manager
x2dJunglist (4:01:35 AM): i mean i know its hard
x2dJunglist (4:01:42 AM): not talking about sexy boys but i mean come ON
lucifer_dramamine (4:01:34 AM): I think we were talking about relationships.. I mentioned how I mailed a package to you
lucifer_dramamine (4:01:36 AM): hahahaha
lucifer_dramamine (4:01:59 AM): but she asked, and I was like, "Yeah, we kinda dated on and off for like a year" and she asked if it ended because you were in japan
x2dJunglist (4:02:21 AM): and you were like
x2dJunglist (4:02:31 AM): "fuck that"
lucifer_dramamine (4:02:10 AM): ha brian I said "No, he's in japan because it ended"
lucifer_dramamine (4:02:12 AM): haha.
lucifer_dramamine (4:05:16 AM): I suck.

XxLUCYS_LIGHT_DREAMxX   [entries | archive | friends | userinfo]

cw/gw in bio

[userinfo | livejournal userinfo]
[archive | journal archive   ]

trip   [July 14, 2005 | 12:15 am]

mike and i are tripping in my room. we laid outside touching
grass as the sun set, as everything went on happening. now
i sit and type while we listen to music. i've been thinking a
lot, a lot a lot, about this buddhism thing, about desire. about
my suffering and its origins and also its persistence. a wish
for something won't get you what you want, but i think it
helps motivate you to put conscious action into your ideal.
it just takes baby steps. the people we idealise is a process
that takes years and years to form, and even then it's not
completely done.

sorry i'm high. as fuclk. on the come up. typing is a bit weird
for me now.

i've been thinking that self improvement is a big joke. because
it too is a hook, it's like "spiritual consumerism." you desire
and desire and keep growing... not that growth is bad. but i
think the desire to constantly reform ourselves into "better
people" is a bad idea because it feeds the feeling that we are
inadequate as we are.

hollow open-echo the future is feeling and i feel it. i think
everything eveything just feels so *right now*. not *right, now*.
but like *right now*. *present*. i dont even think, i keep grabbing
for something thats not there i keep grabbing for something
that is not there. that. it is not there. i and i am open and
feeling and breathing and open everything is so geometric and
manic and beautiful and flowing. cant help but wonder what
i look like righ tnoww.. dfsigj... i love breathing and open..
boundless and free!! i wish right now i am just staring at his
face and its moving but i cant even move my fingers across
the universe

i just can't help but be overwhelmed by the immense beauty
in everything. i wish i could explain the feeling this is echoing
unbroken forever, this is what mike meant when he said
math.... being everything is just meeting as it is and i can feel
it...... i can do this through meditation....

i can't do this typing when the meeting of carbon fingers against the plastic technology feels so foreign and wrong

everything is just so open echoing i cant even explain the meeting of both

***

for a while i was by myself in my room... big mistake. mike went somewhere. i'm trying to recall the confusion i felt. it was like experiencing two different minds, the part of me that likes to suffer and the part of me that wants love.

the frustrating part was not being able to pull them together and not being able to sit still. i felt awful and decided, maybe i will sleep through this feeling and wake up and in the morning i will be okay.

mike came back... he brought candy. he decided to try to being me back up. i became entranced by the symmetry in his hands, playing with the tracers that were dripping off his finger tips. i realized i could create radiance if i thought hard enough and moved his hands in a fashion that brings the ocean against rocky shore lines. this beauty made me ecstatic, like a recreation of realizing that beauty can become a matter of perspective. and that with effort, the perspective can be sustained.

our conversations were like touching the inside and the outside of each other at the same time, saturated with joy and the everything.

***

it seems like everyone seems to think they are so bad at being human. this thought here, shatters the walls of culture apart.

funny that my mind, once so full of thoughts, sits at this keyboard with nothing to say. i am so lost. these words cannot transcribe the way my voice delivers this empathic serenity. through the cosmos, echoing as if nothing were between where my voice is and where it is going.. from my mouth to your ears. now.

the now is what is so beautiful, eternal, this.. fragrant truth, absent, so absent of all symbolic, conceptual thought.. not so much absent as it is complementary. the now is open, boundless, i feel the inside and out simultaneously, it's indescribable. the pain, the crying, oh the crying.. it comes from the reattachment of the past and future onto the now. all is one, but now is now... is this the mushroom talking or is it me? connected with past and future, means there is neither.. just the now. this nonsense, this nonsense that people write only those who have felt can really understand the glistening beauty of ever present boundlessness. its idiotic. its from my buddhist books, too. i get it now. just being.. that's what it was. just to be, let go, giving in to the now. then, the reattachment. the dreary. clinging to the future or the past.. the suffering, that seems so painful.

i want to touch on the meditations.. the light, the light was so.. magnified, it just magnified everything. and my eyes, my eyes were unfeeling, it felt like i was staring so openly.. so open, it felt impossible.

this is not profound truth. but i felt the quiet.. the nothingness.. the vast empty of quiet, so comforting and there and being so fucking aware of it. it was so huge. so large. it was the universe. the quiet was like tapping into the vacuum of the infinite. there was just emptiness.

i just got so fucking lost.

i know i can reach out but i don't make the effort. into the mirror

i just stared. i just stared i just stared and it was just so fucking distasteful. who the fuck am i to do this shit to myself—to starve, to hurt myself like this. i stared futher, closer.. my face.. it became like that face, it did, this strange ever-present face, the four eyes all quaintly, if i tried it, changing into one.. and i stared, i stared into the eye and the darkness, the black center was so vast, so empty, it felt like a hollow core and my iris was just a staggered wasteland encircling the hollowed core.

there are things that seem to be arising as common themes within this thread of laughter.. the thread that fractals downward. i mean i have been known to worship the fractal nature of trees but to actually feel and be math moving?

shit. its strange because i felt like math but the vastness
was something i experienced as an observer. if i let myself
observe.. things.. got very.. empty but also full. i love
the radiant radiating undulating sparkulating.. glimmer of
breathing.

mike is calling me now to the bed.

profound realizations of beauty? there are forks in the road
here... the grandest thing is to exist between the walk and the
talk, for my presence here connects them both and thus they
become one.

XxLUCYS_LIGHT_DREAMxX   [entries | archive | friends | userinfo]

cw/gw in bio

[userinfo | livejournal userinfo]
[archive | journal archive   ]

be the monk   [July 15, 2005 | 8:03 am]

craving is the root of all sufferingthe
self is an illusion which reinforces craving
emotions are a projection of the self
happiness is an emotion
therefore happiness leads to suffering

XxLUCYS_LIGHT_DREAMxX   [entries | archive | friends | userinfo]

cw/gw in bio

[userinfo | livejournal userinfo]
[archive | journal archive   ]

septic   [July 15, 2005 | 12:23 pm]

my mind will be an empty cavity. i remove "obsessions, dogmas, biases."

i will still all processes,

relinquish the substrata of existence,

for the extirpation of craving,

for dispassion,

for cessation,

for extinction.

[comments disabled for this post]

XxLUCYS_LIGHT_DREAMxX   [entries | archive | friends | userinfo]

cw/gw in bio

[userinfo | livejournal userinfo]
[archive | journal archive   ]

tank   [July 16, 2005 | 02:45 am]

only the weak purge
you must be strong
enough to stomach
your mistakes spent
ten minutes repeating
humility liturgy
manic crying to
myself why crying
like a tool must cut
must cut to pay
penance for
gluttony look at
your protruding
stomach as it aches
breakfast at denny's
five donuts rolls of
white bread bowls
of sugar cereal
with a banana (not
yours) donuts from
the gas station a
large slice of
chocolate cake
from the grocery
store a large cookie
four chocolate
covered graham
rackers (not yours)
a snickers bar reese's
peanut butter cups
an entire bag of
fritos and a tub of
five layer bean dip
a half-gallon of milk
1/4 tub of margarine
(to go with the bread)
cheese (not yours) in
the past 32 hours
purged half of this

the other half stomached
i give up body was
83.2 saturday morning
no longer and i am
sick with hum of
anxiety the desire to
split my intestines
open with pressure
to hiccup the diaphragm
and release gallons of chyme into the netherworld of my
house's septic tank the throat this diamond shell my shadow
sees shoulders lurching as i bereave pearly beads of bread in
a chokehold why wish i could be angles and sharp lines when
softness is what pulls people in crave for some dominant
thing to make me love myself since i am powerless against
my own intensity focused inward bruised knuckles against
the soft palette of my own vermillion mouth casts shadows in
my underwear as organs rot out of me tongue bleeds insides
clot out of "me" me the identity the gender specific vulgarity
indifference my preference and so i bleed

XxLUCYS_LIGHT_DREAMxX

[entries | archive | friends | userinfo]

cw/gw in bio

[userinfo | livejournal userinfo]
[archive | journal archive   ]

who am i?

[July 17, 2005 | 12:01 pm]

you are a series of attachments that won't let go. there is no
ego, no self, no identity. there is only the void.

XxLUCYS_LIGHT_DREAMxX   [entries | archive | friends | userinfo]

cw/gw in bio

[userinfo | livejournal userinfo]
[archive | journal archive   ]

connection   [July 20, 2005 | 11:30 pm]

you can't expect every pretty face you come across to be your
next supreme being. but at this point what does it matter. i'm
too scared to get close to Mike, after our shroom adventure
he's been extra clingy and weird and i can't take it.

i'm thinking of giving it up.

but this girl came into radioshack who knows jenny and i can't
stop thinking about her now. she was with her boyfriend, tall,
shaved head, held his hand close. i can't stop thinking about
her sharp eyes and her slouchy jeans and the fairy-tale ends
of that jet-black hair down to her waist.

[current music | look what i did - cupid full of eros]
[6 comments | post comment]

XxLUCYS_LIGHT_DREAMxX   [entries | archive | friends | userinfo]

cw/gw in bio

[userinfo | livejournal userinfo]
[archive | journal archive   ]

-   [July 22, 2005 | 12:05 am]

a piece of thread dangles in my breath
reminds me of a spider's legs dancing
across the curves of sheets.
i can't hide what i feel.

this raw, humanness, you simultaneously
admire and negate it. is it not worth it?
god i was so scared of you, now with good
reason.

i can never find people like you can. maybe that's
what scares me, is that somehow i am less of a
human being, i am, always trying to transcend,
always trying to improve, not so much for you
but it's a good excuse. girls that find you magnetic
are higher, redder, better choices and god
my insecurities are a swarm of locusts,
warm and eating away.

i fight against my judgments,
find my skin too rough
to rub against yours.

the hunger pulls and i remember this feeling.
arms unfold, i fall forward and fingers uncurl like
petals. it's so much less than fresh. i see you in a
new light, distracted eyes.

why do i feel i am doing all the wrong things,
what makes these chemicals attached somehow to yours.

flexibility is a survival tool. as i stretch,
the earthworm casing of my heart breathes with it.

[current music | beloved - vnv nation]
[0 comments | post comment]

XxLUCYS_LIGHT_DREAMxX   [entries | archive | friends | userinfo]

cw/gw in bio

[userinfo | livejournal userinfo]
[archive | journal archive   ]

FUCKk   [July 23, 2005 | 10:54 pm]

the struggle to be together and fit in the right places is driving
me to levels of insecurity i haven't felt in months. we are so
reflective of each other, we just catapult down down down,
each facet of our surfaces shine in ways that keep us blind.
i shield my eyes as the lights fill pores inside of me. i retain,
then leak with the heat, want to feel the radiator ribcage cool
off, cool off from these intensities.

the considerations i've been having say maybe these hearts
beating can't find rhythm, no matter how much mike wills it.
now he's trying so hard, he'll go for days without calling but
the second he wants something he's there. the pieces that
match can't help us fold in half, we break, like thick plastic
with white edges tearing. can't bend back, it only cracks.

so what if maybe i desire the DNA running through my body
to disintegrate into the wells of his tongue, his eyes, his mind
which might be his alone. time spirals quickly, if i don't eject i
might find barbs and wires stuck into my socks down the road,
complications tangled so deep i'm tanked.

problems reeling
i find feelings for him cannot
be unearthed from my skin
the way he shovels down my
back, reaching for some
open portal only
god can find

[current music | tub ring - dog doesn't bite]
[8 comments | post comment]

XxLUCYS_LIGHT_DREAMxX   [entries | archive | friends | userinfo]

cw/gw in bio

[userinfo | livejournal userinfo]
[archive | journal archive   ]

-   [July 26, 2005 | 07:04 pm]

i want to be a cold, steel ball, large enough to be hollow

bells and compartments inside so i sing when i'm moved

cw/gw in bio

[userinfo | livejournal userinfo]
[archive | journal archive   ]

baby this is where my life ends   [July 27, 2005 | 11:11 pm]

her life is sad. i am still too scared to open up about much
but i do talk about past relationships. i talk about mike.
"relationships." years spent searching how to tear my heart
away from my soul and body through sex, accepting that i
will always play second to mothers and girlfriends and wives
because what is wanting when it is coupled by jealousy? can i
even feel that again?

frankie asks, "would you be willing to enter into a relationship
where you're not second or the other woman?"

i think about it.

i say yes.

after four hours, i take her back to her car. i try to be calm, try
to play things off coolly but i was excited that someone this
gorgeous was interested in me. my skin is bad and i'm still
trying to get below XXX pounds. i don't look good.

when i pull up to her car, she stops and turns to me.

she says, "my boyfriend and i, we've been dating for several
years."

she says "we really want to get to know you, but as a couple."

she says "i hope this doesn't change anything between us."

i was ready to reknit myself, i was ready to fuck and feel it for
once.

she puts her hands on mine.

this isn't the first time. a string of problems behind me.

it wasn't that you wanted me. it was that you wanted
something from me.

instead of just being, i have to serve and live on my knees for you, because i know that you will hurt me and this is how i will deal.

coming back to that moment in the car, discussing things. i really try to keep my cool and not let on.

(later she calls, i don't answer, and her voicemail notes i was strangely calm about what she told me.)

in the car, she leaves me on the note of telling her boyfriend about her interest in me.

apparently he is some kind of tattoo artist. we make plans to meet, all three of us, at their place. jenny said they were chill. frankie tells me she would not make me lesser but i know from experience and from my own dynamic that this is not possible. in the car, she holds me and wants to touch me. the warmth calls me and i go to it.

i kiss her and feel like a joke.

cw/gw In bIo

[userinfo | livejournal userinfo]
[archive | journal archive   ]

animals   [April 11, 2022 | 11:11 pm]

shocked this journal is still around. is anybody out there?

the saddest part of reading over these entries is realizing how
long and for how often i let people treat me badly.

everyone wants to know if she is happy.

what happened to her, after she was named? for how long was
she sick? should i put a definitive answer on this?

lovesick or just sick sick.

frankie's boyfriend reached out months later after everything
went down, months and months, maybe even a few years
later. there was a night he was alone, after that, when he and
frankie had split up that i'd gone to visit. i was in college, i
think, and he was trying to get into the army but i'm pretty
sure, in his own words, he had anger issues and they wouldn't
let him in at first.

is it a betrayal to the story to go there? i walked into his
kitchen where he leaned against a linoleum counter, his
stretched lobes stitched up and bandaged, scar tissue on
the bridge of his nose where a piercing should be. still the
same bullshit blue eyes. he fed beer to his dog. we made
small talk, then moved to the living room. i straddled his lap
on the couch. did i look okay? i had shorter hair then. i had
recovered, was fatter than i felt comfortable with. i don't
remember kissing him—it would be a disservice to say i truly
remember the feeling. but i can remember the last time i
kissed someone and felt that kind of passion. years ago, with
a different man, i felt that hunger. and i can reconstruct that
hunger now, in matt's bachelor apartment, as he moved me
to the floor. i can reconstruct all of the rejection, the feelings
that came rushing back. i can remember, vividly, his hands
squeezing the heels of my feet, rubbing them, the way he
made me touch myself. i can remember his lips on each toe,
thinking about how strange and exciting it was that someone
so dominant to me was now in servitude in this way. how it

started, all those years ago in that single moment in the dark, and how since then, any time i feel afraid of rejection, any time i feel the need to repress myself, that desire flares up loud: my nightmare perv obsessiveness that clings and clings inside my head for days.

in his apartment that night, the itchy carpet against my back, i leaned against my elbows and looked at his face there, between my thighs. i rubbed the soles of my feet on his chin, brushed against his lips, wet with spit. he made eye contact with me and suddenly, i got overwhelmed. i couldnt share myself this way. not again. i left. out of fear, as always, of being hurt.

can anyone be cured of this?

there was never another chance to see him again.

my heart hurts for the girl who was afraid to love. some parts of her now feel like a stranger to me. i let that man sit inside, for a moment, in the stretch between my ribs. i wanted gentleness, but he reached too deep. his marks stayed in me. clawing. i was left to crawl towards those open wounds as a way out of my suffering. to form and reform.

maybe thats what it is to trust a person. to let them touch the soft spots when you know that they can wound you. and to do it again, and again, until the scar tissue cords around the nerves, leaving you dead to anything else.

a fire rises in my chest but leaves an empty cavity. that's the sense of it, that's what it is. it is dispossession. the root of suffering is in there, and i know it. the grief of us. the distillation of want into dispassion, as a spiritual effect of loss. as if someone was supposed to be there all along and this whole time i've ignored it, not knowing who it was.

the old me would say it was him. but i know it's not the truth.

i know now, after years of this, it was me.

[comments have been disabled for this post]

ACKNOWLEDGMENTS

between 2003 and 2010 i was part of a community of people with eating disorders on livejournal; one of them started the group ed_ucated because her/our goal was to dispel the idea of pro-ana as something that was normal for people with eating disorders; we also wanted to push out and push away any people who were thinking of experimenting with pro-ana by educating them about the realities of life with an eating disorder. it was a complicated place to inhabit— to both actively pursue your addiction while also warning and even ridiculing 'wanarexics'; wanna-be-anorexics. i think the culture of it inadvertently created a hierarchy of who had a 'real' eating disorder and who didn't. naturally, eating disorders thrive on competition and secrets. but frankly, that community and that exposure allowed me to examine my eating disorder from a more multi-facted mindset. i was sick but i was also able to explore more about why it may have developed, the science behind my sickness, in a way i might have never been exposed to. in effect it launched me into a stream of self-analysis i'm grateful for today. that ability to examine my choices and actions within the context of my physiology or mental make up is eventually what helped me recover. though i've always personally maintained recovery is more like 'health management' than anything else. i'm at such a better place now. it's not like it's perfect with regard to self worth, but the trap i was in during that time is much less opaque.

this book is a work of fiction. yet i continuously think about this community's net positive effect on my life, and how i'm grateful for it. i don't care what people have to say about the dangers of it if they never were in it. i needed that community.

i am still thinking about brett, sarah, lenora, colleen, em, julie, veronica, there are too many to name, but these people provided friendship to me during the darkest period of my adolescent development. i learned so much about myself and the world in the process and about how a person could live their lives. i dislike when people discount the lives of teenagers as dull and that 'everything is dramatic' because we all lived through some traumatic shit and were dealing with it the best we could, we were living through abandonment and abuse and addiction completely on our own with only our fucked up sense of 'rules' to guide us.

i am still friends online with a small handful of the people i met back in those days, though of course through the veneer now of social media which is not nearly as intimate and is much more highly contrived than our livejournals. though i can't say all of us got out of our suffering alive, and i've lost contact with some, and though i do feel that suffering of some kind is always inevitable and permanent, i am grateful the people i'm still in contact with are pushing through life, like, we've fucking made it, bitches. we made it. thank you for being there during that time, thank you for helping make me, thank you for helping keep me alive, thank you for your friendship. i learned who i was in part because of who we all were when we interacted online.

further thank yous go to christoph and leza for being a bang up team of editors on this project and allowing me the freedom to get weird and experimental, to joel for his amazing eye and interior design, thank you to dusty neal for your always impeccable music taste for every right moment, including this one, thank you to kacy dahl and amanda mcneil for being early readers and telling me this project was actually good, thank you to j. david osborne and dusty neal and b.r. yeager for their love of numetal and contributions to the 'current music' section, thank you forever to tom spanbauer, the godfather of dangerous writing, thank you to elizabeth ellen for being the best friend and mentor. thank you to my husband, who helped me during the years-long process of recovery. the most intense thank you goes to my child who is a gift and my greatest motivator. i love you. i would be a different person without you, and i will always be here for you.

ELLE NASH

Elle Nash is the author of the novel *Animals Eat Each Other* (Dzanc Books), which was featured in the 2018 June Reading Room of O - The Oprah Magazine and hailed by Publishers Weekly as a 'complex, impressive exploration of obsession and desire.' A small collection of stories, *Nudes*, is forthcoming from SF/LD Books in 2021. Her short stories and essays appear in Guernica, The Nervous Breakdown, Literary Hub, The Fanzine, Volume 1 Brooklyn, New York Tyrant and elsewhere. She is a founding editor of Witch Craft Magazine and a fiction editor at both Hobart Pulp and Expat Literary Journal.

ALSO BY ELLE NASH

ANIMALS EAT EACH OTHER (Dzanc Books, 2018)

ANIMALS EAT EACH OTHER (404Ink, 2019)

NUDES (Short Flight/Long Drive Books, 2021)

WHAT ARE YOU
Lindsay Lerman

DARRYL
Jackie Ess

WATERFALL GIRLS
Kimberly White

LIFE OF THE PARTY
Tea Hacic-Vlahovic

GIRL LIKE A BOMB
Autumn Christian

PSYCHROS
Charlene Elsby

BURN FORTUNE
Brandi Homan

CENOTE CITY
Monique Quintana

WE PUT THE LIT IN LITERARY
clashbooks.com

 @clashbooks  @clashbooks  /clashbooks

Email
clashmediabooks@gmail.com